I'm Sorry Juno

Belinda Tobin

I'm Sorry Juno

Copyright © 2024 by Belinda Tobin

Published by Bel House Books

Paperback ISBN: 978-1-7637062-4-8

EBook ISBN: 978-1-7637062-5-5

For permissions or enquiries, please contact:

Bel House Books

Email: bhb@heart-led.pub

Website: www. heart-led.pub/bel-house-books

First Edition: October 2024

A catalogue record for this book is available from the National Library of Australia

Other titles from Bel House Books:

The Love Life of a Chameleon

To The Heart of the Man

The Emptiness Algorithm

Crucifixus

I acknowledge the Yuggera and Ugarapul peoples as the Traditional Owners of the lands and waterways where this book was written. I honour the wisdom that lives within the cultures of our First Nations peoples and celebrate its continuity. I pay my deep respects to Elders past, present and future and send my greatest gratitude for all they do for the life of this land.

Always was, always will be.

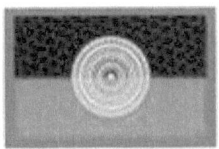 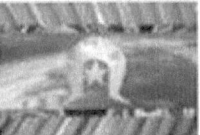

I do not know who this book will reach, or how it will be received. I only know it has been sent with love.

A Note to Readers

This book contains references to sexual abuse, which may be distressing for some readers. These elements are included with care and respect, as they are essential to the themes and messages explored in this work.

If you find yourself feeling overwhelmed or affected by the content, please know that support is available. You are not alone, and there are people ready to help.

Here are some resources you can reach out to for assistance:

United States and Canada: 988 Lifeline — Call or text 988

United Kingdom: Samaritans — Call 116 123

Australia: Lifeline Australia — Call 13 11 14

New Zealand: Lifeline New Zealand — Call 0800 543 354 or text 4357

Chapter 1

I am sitting on the bed where I first met Secret, watching the reenactment of her creation. Like a true crime series, the scene playing out before me has been edited for dramatic effect. The small girl in her school uniform enters the room, but the image is hazy; the identity concealed to protect the innocent. Still, the dress is all too familiar; the maroon gingham is ingrained in my psyche. The camera pans downwards to the girl's basic brown shoes and fallen-down socks as they shuffle forward in slow motion. Another set of shoes, black and much larger than the girl's is shown following close behind. The ominous music begins.

I cannot see the girl's face. The camera will not rise to reveal it. Or is it that I don't want to look? But I don't have to. I know it is mine.

I also cannot see the other's face, only his hand locking the door. Yet I can feel it's singular focus. The other is eager to offer instructions and elicit compliance with its experiments.

Then, there are only sinister snippets between wide intervals of white noise.

The longing.

The loneliness.

The attention.

The anxiety.

Underpants down.

Face down.

The burnt orange bedspread shifts from sending out a warning to offering warmth.

The girl senses a piece of someone else put within a part of her.

That is how Secret came to be.

And Secret is here now.

But I cannot see her full shape. Secret is shrouded in the mist of Memory. To fill the void, I have constructed a story around her, but I have yet to learn how much is fact and how much is fiction. However, while the details of Secret are sparse, I have a solid sense of the sadness she brings.

For Secret is not in the nature of fairy tales or a sublime surprise. She has none of the giddiness that comes with sharing a generous gift. The secret that sits with me here does not waft warm notes of lavender and rose nor whisper about the wondrous thing to come. My secret hangs heavily and drags me downwards. She decorates every success with shadows and invades every intimate encounter. Secret skulks silently in every sentence, ever threatening to expose herself. She smells of disease and sin and radiates disgust.

If it is Secret's will to drive me mad, then she is very close to succeeding. I spend my days clutching at clouds, hoping that one day I will hold onto something solid. Still, I am the one left in a lesser position. Secret knows far more about me than I do about her, but she will not share her power. I want nothing more than to transform my thoughts into truths and meet Secret on equal terms.

I wish I could say that Secret only visits me in this place, this space and time. I could cope if Secret only stayed in the place of her conception. If that were the case, I could simply leave and live freely until my return. Or I could lay waste to the house and be done with the torment forever. But Secret, like a parasitic tick, has burrowed herself within the bloody walls of my heart. There is nowhere I go, nothing I do where she is not.

Secret has also brought a companion to camp beside her. Where this secret goes, Shame surely follows. The two are inseparable invaders.

Shame is the ghost guarding the exits I could use to evict my secret. Whenever I steel myself to share my story Shame stands firm, securing Secret's superiority. Then, Shame shows the destruction that opening the door of speech would ensue. It reveals a community, wailing and crying, with one clear cause.

In the scene Shame presents, the boy's mother clutches at her chest, holding in a heart bursting from the stress. Pain flows from every fibre of her being, for she failed in her duty to raise a respectful boy. My father is there too, and falls, unable to withstand the force of knowing he did not protect his daughter. My sister's back bends further, with this news adding more responsibility and resentment to her already weighty load. There is no celebrating this act of courage and no congratulations for the one who has created this carnage.

There are days I feel callous and willing to condemn others to this fate. But, if I dare to take a step forward, Shame snarls and shakes his finger, reminding me that I walked willingly into the room. How can it be abuse when underneath I was yearning for attention? I allowed it, even encouraged it, and never tried to stop it, so I hold well over half the blame. I am no victim but a participant, and I will be judged as such. Shame knows that this will stop me.

I am well aware that blaming oneself for abuse is a common condition, but also runs counter to the real source of responsibility. "It is not your fault," the experts say matter-of-factly, but words only skim the surface. The sense that I am to blame for this secret is submerged way beneath my skin. It is woven into who I am.

Even if I am willing to move forward and take the blame, Shame educes that there is no evidence for the accusations I allege. The haziness of the happenings certainly does not help. Memory makes a definitive case impossible. Shame shows me being interviewed by detectives, declaring that "I don't know". My responses to their repeated questions are riddled with "I think" and "I may have". At this point, the video of proceedings is paused, and Shame carefully explains how such language is often evidence of a lie. It is a sign of the suspect shaping the story as they go along, and being unwilling to commit to actions they may need to alter.

Then the inspector asks who can corroborate my version of events; who can validate my victimhood? There is no-one, and I am left to sit and stew in my own self-doubt, while Shame sniggers by my side.

Unsatisfied, Shame goes further, suggesting that with my track record of mental illness, parents, aunts, uncles, siblings, and spouses will likely laugh this story off as just the latest chapter in a life of lunacy.

It is true that the first half of my life was spent surprising strangers with stories that made me sound far more interesting than my real life would allow. The "I" I was seeking was not limited by imagination and I created many fantastical characters that would impress my colleagues and attract guys at the clubs. Since then though, things have become a lot more serious. I have collected multiple definite diagnoses and had several dramatic admissions to psychiatric facilities. This story then, if I were to share it, would be viewed as just another indicator of my instability. Secret would be seen as another example of my unbalanced state. I wonder what it would take for it to be recognised in its rightful place, not as a creation from my chaos, but as the cause, the source of my sickness.

Every plan I develop to deport Secret, involves some risk of worsening my own reputation or hard-fought relationships. Every possible deed has the risk of damning someone I love. In between my bursts of determination, Shame whispers, "Haven't you caused enough hurt already?" With these words, Shame has won, for I know they are true.

In University I put my parents in a wilderness of worry. There was little I could control in this crazy context, but I found one thing I could take charge of - my consumption. I swapped out fears about boyfriends with concerns about calories. I replaced entertainment with exercise. I strived to be skinny and succeeded so very well. No one else shared my ecstasy, though and instead I was put on notice that if I did not improve I would be hospitalised. They thought I was mentally ill. I thought what I was doing was meaningful. They saw me as a patient. I saw myself as powerful.

To get me back on track, my mother came to stay, vacuuming my apartment to exorcise any evil embedded in the environment. She came with me to the raft of medical appointments, sat beside me as I ate and slept with me to make sure the food was kept down. I remember at this time one psych asking me what I thought was wrong with me. Back then, I thought he was an idiot. Now, I think it was nice of him to consider that I may have had that much insight into my internal chaos.

Through much talking and medication, I found an even balance, enough to finally be trusted again. And then, through self-imposed isolation, I found my own way through. I moved to a unit by the sea, walked on the beach and breathed in the salty air. It was the tonic that turned my mind around. I studied hard and slept alone, drifting off to the sound of the waves. I accepted awards and accolades for my academic achievements. And then I cooked cupcakes, cheesecakes, tarts, and tortes, taking them at once to the adopted aunts and grandmothers upstairs, for I could not yet trust myself. Still, around pots of tea and packet coffees I made connections with these wise women, and these connections were crucial to restoring confidence. They showed me that there were parts of me worthy of love.

Then, just as I had regained health and removed the burden of worry on my parents, I took off travelling the world. My journal entries show a muddle of mixed motives. I was both eager to escape some unnamed ghosts and excited to share my energy. On one page I had written, "I love them a lot, but I need to get away." On the next was, "The world is going to be so glad it met me". The innocence and joy in these words still make me smile. Searching for adventures and sharing my spirit seemed to silence Secret for magical moments and gave Shame some time off. I was instead entranced by Buddhism in Thailand, in awe of the simple sophistication in Sweden, captivated by the culture in Russia, and embraced by the community in Ireland. And as I was exploring foreign lands, I was also finding myself.

But for every going out, there is a coming back.

On my return, after the mandatory displays of affection, I was advised that my absence had turned my mother's hair white. I had noticed how she had aged, but now I realised it was my adventure that caused the angst. My delights had caused their distress. And what I considered a success for me was a source of great suffering for them. I guess they were a bit shocked to see me bald; my shaved head resulted from an impulsive act in Italy. And they would have been a bit surprised to see the weight I had gained. I had dropped off anorexia somewhere along the way and picked up a new buddy, bulimia. I was not sure whether my heaviness was accompanied by Hope or simply more heartache.

But even this friend was dumped when I set off for Sydney, headed for the big smoke to start my career. The pain was plastered over with pride and bandaged with brand-new briefcases and business suits. I wore a consultant's badge but soon realised, in this company, they were only pleased when the pin pierced the skin. Every day I felt like I was being pried out of my shell, only to be smothered, smashed, shrunken, and shoved back into a sharp, ill-fitting one. I persevered because there was a silver lining; saving my salary for more adventures abroad.

Every one of my trips provided a new perspective, be it on the crowded streets of China, the sparkly seas of Portugal or the mountainous mists of central America. My time upriver on the Amazon showed me how much I felt at home, alone in nature. However, this lesson, while a gift, became a curse on my return.

For every going out there is a coming back.

My first day back at work I was carried off a crowded train by a tide of people. I could not breathe amidst this mass and so sat down to regain a sense of composure. As I did I watched waves of people make their way up the escalators. One wave was followed by another, then another, and then two would converge and come crashing together on the concourse. As time passed, the surges up the stairs dwindled in intensity but were relentless in their continuity. Then and there, my childhood dream of meeting every person in the world was exposed as a fool's errand. I felt completely alone.

The despair opened the door for more self-destruction. I spent nights in drunkenness and debauchery, which I conveniently explained away as curiosity and a practice of self-compassion. I searched for new worlds down dark alleys and for a community in the chaotic hearts of Kings Cross. My days were spent as a consultant, dressed for success, in a body one boyfriend described as perfect for a Botticelli painting; my downtime was spent in alcohol and adult adventures. I was on a mission to determine if there was a devil. On this crusade, I sacrificed nice men for the chase of impossible prizes, honesty for the mask of heroism and self-respect for being able to say that I had tried everything once.

A blessing came with a posting to Brisbane. Boarding in the city, I was free to walk and to wander. The space and slower speed were soothing, and I could feel myself settling. The agitation and self-flagellation were replaced with friendship, fidelity, meeting families, a shared flat and finances, and finally, the role of a fiancée. I revelled in my newfound ability to take the form of normal. My mother was not well enough to watch my father walk me down the aisle. Still, she celebrated my stability from her hospital bed. She was dying and yet found the strength to smile, raising a toast to the happy couple. Her pain was placated by the thought that I had a husband to help me through the impending grief.

Grief though was not something I got through. In fact it festered into alcohol addiction and more damning diagnoses. My father had to bear these alone and this thought causes me so much anguish. For years, he held fragile hopes for my recovery, offering them out with love, only for me to throw them callously to the floor. Repeated stints in rehab and psych hospitals also left my husband harrowed. With mindlessness came many indecent actions, and with hangovers came even more self-hate. I was coached in self-compassion and made confident commitments to medication. However, words were easy, actions much harder. Self-care came second to spraying shame over those I professed to love. With each binge, I swept any remnants of trust and security into the bin. My beautiful little girls became the innocent victims of my internal war, one that created so much carnage.

The experts gave a name to the enemy embedded within. It was borderline personality disorder, a verdict both vague and vulgar. At forty-three, it was a diagnosis that came far too late. But supposedly, its patterns only become clear after decades of diabolical damage. I had never stayed in one place long enough to have someone piece the puzzle together. And I had not previously granted anyone permission to see the full picture, even myself.

I was advised that expelling the enemy would take years of expensive treatment. I began, but my bank account could not sustain the price of peace. However, I had been set up with enough knowledge to negotiate a treaty on my own terms. Instead of returning to group sessions, I separated from my husband and retreated to connect with myself. I set up my own sanctuary, a place I could call my own, and one that was safe and sustaining for my girls. Of course, my psych did not see it quite the same, suggesting it was just another example of my preference for running away. However, I know this move was not about seeking distraction but deep knowledge. And I have learned for myself one thing that my psych was either unwilling to believe or loathe to reveal, that the sickness he scribbled on his sheet was only a symptom. There was something much deeper driving my self-destruction. All the digging I have done over the past years has brought so much awareness, but it has also exhumed the excruciating secret that stands before me.

And now Shame also seeks to taint my sanctuary. It reminds me that I have not been here to help my father when he is hurting. My sanctuary is presented as a selfish solution to avoid doing a daughter's duty. I have stayed away from my father's suffering, and my absence has made me a traitor.

While those who supported me were waging their own war, I was alone, soaking up the warmth of the sun and the spirit of trees and perfecting the practice of self-care.

But for every going out there is a coming back.

Shame has made one thing clear for me. That is, I cannot share Secret with my father. It would surely kill him. My other depravities caused him despair, but this one would cause his death. If I ever was going to, it should have been done years earlier, when he was strong enough to survive the shock or maybe even snap the neck of his nephew, and where there was time for me to make it right.

Yes, Shame would have great fun working on someone so vulnerable. My father worked so hard to provide things for me that were impossible for him. But Shame would not let reality interrupt the casting of blame. He would shout scoldings at my father and state that his absence opened the opportunity for abuse. Shame would pummel the poor man with the belief that he did not provide proper protection, and so was a pathetic excuse for a paternal figure. Shame would ensure my father's last moments would be filled with torment.

No. My father holds no fault for the birth of Secret, and he should not have to hold more hurt. And yet, Secret has stolen so much. Someone must pay for providing it with the privilege.

That someone is my cousin, and I am coming to terms with the inevitable need to confront him. He is the co-creator of Secret and so must take some of my blame. I know I will feel better when this burden is lighter. But this is where I am stuck. I still need to know the true shape of Secret for it is unlikely that my cousin will be honest. I need to know what he did, exactly what he did before I can cast stones. I cannot accuse until I am assured of the actual actions he took. But Secret has been swirling around, hidden in the mist of Memory for many years. I have spent so much energy trying to pull pieces of the puzzle from the ether and to gather evidence. And yet, I am still lost.

There is one person, though, who could help. I don't even know if they exist, but I have read enough to know that the presence of angels is plausible. I believe there is much more going on around us than we can see; that we are ignorant of what is invisible. And it cannot be denied that there was a presence at mum's death, guiding and supporting me from above. If it is true, and I do have a Guardian Angel, then it would have been here, in this room. It would have witnessed the creation of Secret and hold the truth in detail. This angel would not be limited by the manipulations of Memory. Yes, Angel has the power to resolve my problem. Angel will have the answers I want. Now I just have to find Angel.

Still, there is a sense of discomfort progressing down this street to find my solution. Firstly, it just sounds stupid; relying on an angel to resolve childhood trauma. But then when has the rationality of any remedy ever been a barrier before? Surely searching for a compassionate deity is a better choice than continued self-flagellation? Besides, there are more critical issues to deal with. Because if Angel was there witnessing the creation of these wounds, why didn't it intervene? Why didn't it prevent Secret from taking shape? Perhaps there is some angel code that must allow acts of free will. If so, this is truly ghastly. For in abiding by this code, the angel would have preferred the will of a predator over the wellbeing of a child. Angel would have known the decades of distress that its inaction would cause. So, did it choose to allow my crisis out of simple conformance to commandments? If this is the case, my adviser will be no angel but decidedly a devil in disguise.

Even though, and giving Angel the benefit of the doubt, if it was not able to act as my protector, did it then, and does it now, share my pain? Does Angel see the suffering Secret causes and the doubt I live each day? Does it follow behind me also bearing the weight of the wrongs? Does Angel feel regret for being unable or unwilling to remedy the situation? Does Angel feel remorse for all the hurt it has allowed?

If so, then Angel needs to give me a goddamn apology.

Perhaps also, Angel has foresight into the future. In that case, it could help reacquaint me with Hope.

Either way, it would be nice to have an angel here to sanctify this space and to pass on some peace to my father. Dad's snoring is shaky now, which I find so sad. In my younger years, I considered the thunderous sound that would echo down the halls disgusting and selfish. Tonight, it is far better than silence, for it, at least, is a sign of life.

I'M SORRY JUNO

Chapter 2

I searched for Angel in the online world for about an hour, and there were some promising pathways. One site, after receiving my email address, supplied me with a name of who my Guardian Angel was; however, I could not pronounce it let alone pray to it. Yet, for a small monthly fee I could be sent much more detail and daily messages from a raft of divine entities. I declined the kind offer and promptly unsubscribed from their mailing list. Of course, they were sorry to see me go, and so was my angel. I then found a psychic, who, for a considerable sum, was willing to sketch my angel and supply me with a picture. My inner sceptic shut this option down quickly, surmising it would be simply generated by AI, and I could do this all by myself. I could create my own angel if I was that way inclined. Then I was offered the ultimate package. If I was willing to make a substantial financial investment, payable in monthly instalments, I could get someone I don't know to communicate with Angel on my behalf. Every month a medium would petition my Guardian Angel to provide specific direction for the weeks ahead, providing clarity on how to deal with my daily challenges.

I fell asleep lamenting the crimes of commercialism. Yes, there may be honest vendors out there, who have simply decided to offer their services through different doorways. Yet from my small exploration, it was easy to see how the open social media market invites in all manner of spiritual scammers. They prey on our laziness and longing, our ache for answers. They offer the opportunity to outsource hope. And they profit from our comfort in being incompetent with the invisible. Judging the stupidity of others in handing over their cash came easily. At the same time, I knew if I came across anything credible, I, too, would be entering my credit card number.

Given the amount of blue light I would have absorbed, the continual concern for my father, and the challenging context, I had not expected to sleep. So, I awoke with a start and sped to check on my father. He was still breathing and appeared comfortable. After a small chat I went to make tea, and that is when Shame came to stand beside me. How could I rest when dad was dying in the next room? How could I look for angels when he was in such anguish? Shame put it simply, I was a bad daughter and my Mother, God bless her soul, would be saddened by such selfish behaviour. Shame's words stung and yet I knew the reality with which I was faced. Years of practice in facing pain had allowed me to become adept at dissociation. My psych stated definitively that it was a maladaptive behaviour that required a remedy. But he does not seem to understand it was also a protector and one I became to rely upon.

Detachment may become helpful today too, as I spend my time trapped within this little cottage; once built for my grandparents, but now my father's final home. The house dad built for his own dependents, my mother, my sister and brother, is only one block away, but is off-limits to me. My sister lives there with her children, coming home to care for my mother through her traumatic illness, and staying after her death. Dad could not deal with the wars that came with living with his child, so he moved to the cottage to live simply and calmly.

And, after years of wounding my sister with intoxicated words, I am no longer welcome in what was my childhood home. I understand. I didn't want me around back then, either. She had every right to prevent her home from being soiled with my self-destruction and contaminated by my sickening condition. She was doing her duty to let my mother's ghost rest there in peace and secure her children's safety. However, we both knew that my excessive and excruciatingly selfish behaviour was not the only reason for my exile. It was not a lone event but the final straw in a separation that had started when I was six. The estrangement began well before I became a drunkard; it was an evolution from the conflict that was created when we were children.

My sister has come to visit dad regularly while I have been here. With our father she is pragmatic and supportive. With the visiting doctors and nurses, she is cordial and decisive. With me she is perfunctory and practically speechless, perfected from years of practice. Any conversation is concise, focused on facts and avoiding anything fragile. This is nothing new. Family was never a place for sharing of feelings. You wouldn't want those closest to you thinking you were faulty.

I spent the day being busy, coordinating the constant parade of my father's supporters in and out of the cottage. The care I took to prepare tea, coffee and cake for the visitors was a delightful distraction from the reason they had called in. The smell of the home-made scones and sugary beverages was a sweet respite from reality. And when my Aunt asked to see some photos of my girls, there were smiles and praise aplenty, saving us all from being sucked into the sombreness.

In our alone moments, my father would sleep and I found silent pursuits, ones that would not disturb. However, I also wondered whether the sound of basic household chores would be more reassuring. He spent his life with the television on in the background, and after mum died, the radio was always babbling beside his bed. The clash of conversations would always drive me crazy, but he seemed to gain comfort from the continuous company. I wondered; would the absence of activity now merely be causing him more anxiety? And if so, why would I be allowing this to happen? How dare I force more discomfort upon him when he is already dealing with death? I despaired at not having the wisdom to know what he needs right now, and he has no energy to waste on such menial contemplations. So, I just continued, checking in periodically to see if any insight appeared to guide an intervention.

But I could not concentrate on work; my clients would have to wait. I do not deliver second-rate solutions; and this is neither the time nor place for productivity or perfectionism. Writing about unrelated matters felt disrespectful, and all topics felt trivial. I know my father would disagree, always determined to complete work commitments no matter the toll or torment they would demand. I had no doubt that he would be relieved by the thought that I was sitting in the lounge room delivering something deemed important; a document to help someone make a crucial decision or an invoice that would pay the next round of school fees. But right now, for me, it all feels like a fanciful fuss and a misguided use of my time.

So instead, I made my way to the mantelpiece and embarked on a new assignment; not one of action, but of attention. I had never taken the time to look, really look at the pictures upon it. Sure, I had glanced between going from one room to the next, but I never stopped to look behind the smiles. Standing here, staying here, felt right, like I was being called to connect, beyond the images, to the individuals beneath.

I see dad, standing beside his own, so energetic and excited to be on the shop-front sign as a 'son'. He was the only one. There was no choice. But I can see the pride in his eyes at the public recognition. He looks still like the lanky larrikin I have heard about, finding fun in masculine mischief. Here, he is replacing rebelliousness with responsibility and reducing his world to take on this role. Yet his love of laughter has never left him. He looks like he could tell a good yarn back then, just as now he gets boundless joy from sharing a joke. And there he is upon his horse playing polocrosse. What a magnificent creature, and what a powerful pursuit. How much skill and danger were involved, and how much courage to charge along on such a beast and catch a ball. What trust my father must have placed in his mount, his teammates and how much comradeship would have been forged through this folly. I can't remember seeing my father play, but I recall helping out in the canteen as a child, and dancing at the disco afterwards. I still think so fondly of the man who helped me work out the change at the cash register; his calmness and encouragement gave me confidence. And then there was the lady who carried me out onto the dancefloor for a "boogie". Even now, whenever I hear 'Eagle Rock,' I get a sense of feeling wanted, of feeling whole.

There is dad again, in this photo with less hair and a larger waistline. He stands smiling beside my brother, who is bearing an award. And again, he is there beaming beside my sister dressed as a debutant. Following along the mantle, I find dad proudly beside me as I wore the mandatory white gown for graduation. I sense a weariness and worry already well ingrained, but also a sense of relief that his efforts were providing some reward.

These photos are informative, but I know they only hold selective memories. Between each image, there is an interval. And I can't help but contemplate the prints that were not taken for fear of those times never being forgotten. I remember the story dad told of finding a man dead in the house across the road. Hung or shot, I am not sure, but the trauma would be captured in the coroner's files and etched in my father's psyche. Nor do I see here the desperate image of my grandfather huddled on the back step of this house. What we know as depression was seen then as a deficiency, and his tears were not viewed as a sign of humanity but of madness. How much it must have hurt for Nan and dad to see this torment and not know how to help. There are also no photos shown here of my sister dating sinister men. There is not one of our family together with the doctor the day he came to declare my mother's fate, nor any of my brother's debilitating anxiety attacks that followed. I do not see a photo of dad's body crumpled with the pain of spinal damage. And there is not one of me being monitored in a mental hospital or vomiting red wine all over the walls, or the look of disgust on dad's face when he found out I had been drinking. No, I do not see any of these dramas to counter the delights, but that does not mean they did not happen.

I look at dad's face and remember how much he looks like our lauded ancestor, a captain in the colonies and commander of important infrastructure. Once this forebear was ridiculously wealthy and was declared local royalty with the best racehorses to prove it. But he lost it all. The pendulum swung and usurped his power, leaving him penniless. The captain's legacy of a church, cottage and a few street names still exist some kilometres down the road. My dad then never became the descendent of a decadent dynasty. The captain's children had to make their own way. With independence, though, came invention, and dad never ceased to amaze me with his ingenuity. During the day dad was always creating a new piece of machinery or piloting a new process. When the sun set, he would spend the night sketching a new and better version and entering exact measurements. I have come to recognise that this was Creation's way of creeping through; finding ways to thrive in any context.

After the captain's downfall, the lineage never seemed interested enough in God to be involved in the rituals of religion. Apart from Nan cleaning the church next door, I did not see any semblance of spirituality on this side of the family. So, I was not surprised when dad declared his belief that death is an absolute end, that there is nothing more but darkness. I did not know whether he was clinging to or wrestling with this notion right now and I was certainly not going to ask. I only knew that this thought fills me with terror.

How different he is from mum. I would like to know more about how a Protestant and Catholic came to be a couple, and why, despite his religious reservations, he still went with mum to church every Saturday night. After every mass, at least half of the ten siblings from mum's side of the family, would converge on the cement to chat, cackle and share concerns. Aunts and Uncles would discuss the weather and cousins would stand around, uncomfortable in their church clothes and try, as instructed, not to act like children. I could sense the strength mum gained from these congregations; they sustained her. I am sure she must have been shattered when, after so many years, dad confessed his distaste for all the drama and declared his decision that he would no longer attend. Just like that, church was dropped.

Mum, though, never let go of Faith. Where dad had a bedside stash of The Land and Trading Post newspapers, mum had a Bible and rosary beads. The beads are now treasures I keep in my jewellery box. They remind me of something invisible, and yet vitally important. They secure my sense that there is something much more, a superior source of strength. They are blue, her favourite colour and the one she wore to work each day. It is so ironic that she gravitated towards the colour of the throat chakra. Maybe it was to express all that she was not confident enough to set free except when expected through hymns. Or was it to soothe the toxicity that resulted from this repression, which manifested in two thyroidectomies and a lifetime of medication? These beads hold so many messages. In my mind, there are far more magical than mundane. I have no access to any more of mum's tangible memories. These are being well-guarded by my sister as relics in the room of her death, the place where I met Love and received the instruction to pass it on.

I move along to my parents' wedding photo. Mum is beaming beside her bridesmaids, all selected from her many sisters. The brightness of the day that was is now blander, bleached by the hands of time. Mum's cheeks are so rosy that I can't tell whether this was her natural state, or a tint put on by the photographer in post-production. The whole colouring is quite surreal, which, after my own nuptials, I can attest to being an exact portrayal of the aura around the actual event.

I see mum's red hair and hazel eyes and think about the nickname the blokes gave her, Bluey. Knowing mum's gentleness and humour, it would have been a term of endearment applied solely for their entertainment. I did not receive the gift of the recessive red hair, but every now and again, I would honour my heritage with the help of Henna.

In the next photo she stands beside my brother, my sister, and I, smiling with pride. And there she is in the hospital bed with her celebratory glass of apple juice, toasting the wedding of her daughter that she could not attend. I still regret that my speech to the guests that night had not included a request for them to have a dance for my mum and, in their quiet moments, send her love. I don't know why I didn't, but I do remember the sensation of a hand at my heart holding me back. Thinking about it now, I am sure many of them would have sent out subliminal messages of care for my mother anyway. The conversations over champagne would have included concerns about her absence and the certain fate she was facing. There would have been empathy flowing through the ether and directed to her destination. Who am I to think any of these wonderful people needed my guidance to enact their generosity?

I wished then that I had more meaningful photos of mum, which were less of an expected exhibit and more that were evidence of the mother she was. It would be nice to have had a selfie of us headed to my first bra-fitting, an incredibly important rite of passage. It would be great to have some shots of her on one of her Sunday afternoon cooking sessions. After the remnants of the roast lunch were cleared away, out would come the ingredients for cakes, slices, puddings, and pies. Many times, while tying myself in knots trying to replicate this perfect role model, I wish I had pictures of her harrowing humanity. Like the tears she shed when she shared her fears of my father's infidelity. Like the angry outbursts that were out of her control thanks to hormones gone haywire. Like the grief expressed at her mother's funeral. And like the look on her face when she found out she would only be with us for a few more months. To cherish a picture of your mother's corpse would be viewed by some as clear proof of a crazy mind, and yet it would be one of the most profound. Because I don't want to have these photos to worship her misery. I want them as a reminder that it is possible to shine through suffering and to still give so much through your own grief.

If eyes are the window to the soul, I wish I could see more clearly into my mother's; to discern the details. When she was first diagnosed with Motor Neuron Disease, out of sheer desperation, I sent her photo to a psychic. I hoped to understand the cause of this catastrophe and find a way to cure it. What the seer saw was unsettling. There was a fog over some experience with her father, like a cataract clouding her consciousness. There was a fugue interrupting her vision and vitality. The psychic gave a healing from a distance, but nothing more could be done from outside of herself.

A thunderbolt jolted me out of my thoughts. Its rumbling ended with the echo of a voice I heard long ago.

"You look like the spitting image of your mother."

This idea was disturbing so I departed, creating distance from the photos and checking on dad. However, on my way back to the kitchen, curiosity took hold, and I stopped in the tiny bathroom and stared into the small mirror. Honestly, I couldn't see that much of a resemblance. As I child, I thought that the only thing we shared was a middle name. Sure, I have her hair. And now I also understand how one can be too busy for curl care. I too, share the frizz I used to frown upon. I don't remember my mother with so many wrinkles though. My face is woven with them, fine lines, crow's feet, deep etchings, and dry crinkles. They cease only at the saggy eyelids, which I suspect will soon need surgical correction.

With all this activity on my face, it is easy not to notice the absence of eyebrows. I had never known of this deficiency until a sassy nail artist looked me in the eye and screeched through her nostrils, "What happened to your eyebrows, girlfriend?" I spent the rest of the session trying to ignore her repeated suggestion that I should have them tinted or tattooed on. But back home that night, I could see what she meant. There was not much there at all. A small tuft of a darker shade at the centre which disappeared dramatically into sparse, see-through strands. They look like someone had been silly enough to try and shave them off but got distracted halfway through.

My girls have a good giggle at my expense and goad me to get my eyebrows "done". I did once but felt even more self-conscious with big brown bangers on my face. To this day, though, it is the one thing I am drawn to on a person's face. I am constantly driven to understand just how dramatically mine differ. I will not admit to ogling. I merely observe. There is no lechery in my looking. I take no joy in judgment but will admit to taking some comfort in criticising those who have chosen to have them drawn on. I don't quite understand the value in me that it violates, but I find them vulgar.

My browlessness, though, is far more than interesting, it is ironic. I am named after Juno, the Queen of the gods and the mother of Mars, who, for some strange reason, felt compelled to care for the eyebrows of all women. From what I can understand, it was because they were the outward representation of the woman's vitality, her spirit, and the goddess within that would travel with her for life. Juno would provide the protection each woman needed so they could find the goddess within and let it shine. She would ensure they had a sufficient lintel to bear the load of the life that would come down upon them and shield their precious soul.

Well, whatever the reason, from my bare brow, it can be deduced that my namesake gave up watching over me and stopped trying to secure my soul. Perhaps the original Juno was peeved that I dared to denigrate her name and so she decided to abdicate any further responsibility, shown by my receding brow. I certainly have not given her much to celebrate. Or maybe it was I that cast her away when I decided no singular being, either on earth or in heaven, could be trusted. I afforded her no special privilege in this process of exclusion. With Juno gone, joy could also simply slip away, and this sparsity is now expressed clearly above my eyes.

I cannot conclude whether a Juno with no eyebrows is hilarious or horrific, a comedy or a tragedy, merely coincidental or a callous creation.

Later I attend the regular phone appointment with my psych. While only short due to my situation, I still welcome them. During this conversation I could not help but amuse myself. I knew that mentioning this mythology would annoy him, but I went further to suggest it could hold some significant meaning. As always, he asked me to keep this hippie crap for my counsellor, demanding that instead of stupid symbology, we spend our time on the serious matter of my mental health. I told him I was doing as well as can be expected, surrounded by Secret and Shame and my dying dad.

I talked to him about the torment of being unable to remember critical details of what I thought was a crucial time of my life and the opportunity I may have to confront my cousin. But how, first, I feel compelled to clear the confusion.

He reminded me of a concept raised several times before; the dilemma of dissociate amnesia. In my best sarcastic voice, I said, "Sorry, I forgot." He did not find this funny.

He then offered the options for me as he saw them, hypnosis, or acceptance.

I told him that I considered the first hopeless. No matter what was revealed, there would always be doubt. I am well aware of my ability for self-deceit. So, I am unlikely to trust anything from my brain as a definitive answer. In high-school I could look my schoolmates in the eye and tell them that my father was a member of Duran Duran and that I had been billeted to this backwater to ensure a normal upbringing. And in the pubs, I could impress future mates with stories about which part of Sweden I was from, adding a little accent here and there for extra emphasis. For attention, I had told one ex-partner of an abortion. To avoid responsibility at work, I had made up a rape. How could I ever know what was real and what was my immoral imagination at play?

So, I was left with acceptance. Acceptance that it may only ever be dispassionate professionals that I can share my stories with. Acceptance that I may never have a full understanding of those significant years. Acceptance of my feelings of fault. But also, acceptance of the fact that to move forward, I must learn to forgive.

The doctor asked me if I could forgive myself for what happened and for all the years of hurt I caused in its hangover. I replied that I was unsure, which was met with a request for a simple yes or no answer. I had to acknowledge that, no, I was not yet capable of forgiving myself. I was not willing to invite Forgiveness in.

The doctor pulled out the familiar dagger of directness and declared that until I could do this, I would continue to be a danger to myself and others. With that thought, our time was up.

The thunder that followed made the doctor's declaration feel like a threat.

For hours afterwards I sat with my father, listening to the music he loved, holding his cold hand, and watching his breath become less certain and more shallow. I called my sister and brother, who came just in case. As they had their time alone with dad, I sat outside and watched the lightning show. I had always admired lightning's ability to evade predictability and perform unscripted. Its power held a promise of what was possible.

Watching it have fun with its ferocity, I thought about Forgiveness. Could it be the force to shock me out of this stagnation and show me the way? Now knowing how hard it is to be human, Forgiveness was something that I had thought I offered to others freely. But the doctor's words made me wonder; was I really being genuine with my Forgiveness? Was I able to give it fully when I had not first given it to myself? Had my attempts at pardoning others been merely a placebo, missing the active ingredient of integrity? Have my words been just more lies, layering over my lack of understanding of what true Forgiveness entails?

My introspection was interrupted by an intense integration of thunder and lightning, landing before me at the garden gate and resulting in an automatic shriek. I surveyed the space carefully, concerned that sparks may cause a fire. There were no flames, but there was an afterglow. Within it stood two human shapes. From these figures, flowing outward, I could feel the same energy that had sat above my mother's lifeless body and which provided an endless source of purpose.

Yes, Dad, it is a good night to die.

Chapter 3

I was summoned back inside by my sister who said that dad had gone. No cuddles were forthcoming as she charged on to call the doctors and funeral directors. As always, I was left there feeling like the clumsy klutz that was not worth caring for. This crisis was progressing in the same pattern that had plagued our relationship to date; she played the parent and I was the child. It was a script we knew well and had never tried to transcend. I remember her rage on my first day of high school when she had to get off the bus and grab her stupid little sister from the wrong service, saving me from ending up stranded. And when I became anorexic, my parents sent me to stay with my sister in the Northern Territory, knowing that she would quite happily tell me what to do.

At the pub, my sister cajoled me to consume more calories, suggesting that if I had to put on weight, I may as well drink it on, and then ordering another round. I wonder if, years later, and after hanging up from yet another intoxicated conversation, she may have felt apologetic for giving me this advice. I wonder if she was sorry for sanctioning the actions that would be the cause of so much suffering. There were some heartfelt moments during my visit, like when she told me that she was jealous of my charisma and confidence. Perhaps she also became jealous that my form of benumbing was much more daring and dramatic than hers. I often wonder how she felt at my wedding, watching me be showered in confetti while she headed towards old maid status. She had many angry outburst through the night, directed at her small sone, but I could not help but wonder whether I was the intended audience.

I cannot remember a time when we were ever close. Our paths always seemed to cross, never converge. My curiosity about her clothes, jewellery and makeup was a source of contention, not companionship. She never seemed interested in educating me about her grown-up explorations, merely to escape into them. I see a similar streak in my eldest daughter. I am constantly shuttling this teenager between sports and social events and, when she is at home, she is constantly submerged into social media. Stillness and silence are not appreciated.

So, it was inevitable that my sister would set off to make a life far enough away from the family to be interesting and independent. Perhaps she also hoped that freedom of identity would be delivered with distance.

But for every going out, there is a coming back.

My sister's return to take up the responsibility of caring for mum appeared to be a willing one, but there was a base of bitterness that seemed best kept for me. It would erupt at otherwise trivial times. When mum's arms no longer worked, cardigans became a comfort and a challenge. I could never put one on mum in a way that met my sister's superior standard. The words, "I'll do it", masked her contempt at my incompetence and immaturity. Before being banned, I hosted my daughter's christening at the family home and my sister was far from impressed. Here, sausage rolls became the scapegoat. She would not allow the stove to be kept on to keep them warm; I was not worth the extra gas bill. As aunts and uncles, cousins and neighbours converged to celebrate, I clearly saw the contempt she held for me. My sister had two faces, one of sugar, which she showed freely to the guests, and one of spite that she reserved for me.

After the addiction took hold, her animosity seemed to evolve into disgust, evidenced by her inability to even give me a glance. Her distaste was so deep that seeing me was even a step too far. I could not get angry at her actions, for back then I found it impossible to even accept myself. Our roles had reversed; now I was the one who envied her, for she could walk away while I had to keep fighting this war. Eventually, acrimony abated into apathy and a full absence of contact. She retreated behind enemy lines to await my next move, be it full-blown self-destruction or a resolution that may offer the chance of reconciliation.

Our children were innocent victims in this hostility; estranged, only to meet again years later on social media. During visits, I would ask if, at the very least, my children could catch up with their cousins, but my sister always said that they were too busy. It was clear I was considered a threat to her precious progeny, who must be shielded from my selfish sickness. And I did not feel confident to go further afield and cart them around the multitude of extended family members. My girls, then, had a vastly different upbringing from mine. On mum's side, there was a cast of aunts, uncles and cousins that would convene at BBQs and birthday dinners. The women would cook and cackle, and the men would discuss the climate, crops, or cars. And the offspring would stay out of sight, not always out of trouble. I do wish my girls could have experienced such a gaggle. They will soon know a similar gathering, but this one will be tainted by tears.

My brother's eyes were filled with them already, and they were flowing down his face. His huge arms gave the strongest, warmest hug, one from the heart. He was a man of such few words, sharing them only for support, satire, or a sinister combination of both. As a teenager, most of his responses were a few careless grunts that worked to dissuade further questioning. But his voice evolved to provide little sparks of enlightenment. Cleaning the house one day I could not have been bothered moving the lounges to vacuum. His passing remark was, "If you are going to do something, do it well." At the time, I responded to this sage advice with a simple "shut up." Yet, his suggestion has stuck with me.

My brother's humour was always helpful, bringing a positive perspective to the pain. I remember, on one visit, when he asked how I was. After I said I was good, he replied, "Well, you sure look better than the last time I saw you." It was said with a smile, smoothing over the severity of our last meeting. The gathering he referred to was a caucus to confirm dad's care arrangements after yet another operation. The hospital became a battleground. I brought the soldiers of self-harm and sadism, and the shrapnel of red wine was splattered down the walls. It was not blood shed that day, but the last vestige of my self-respect. Little did I know, but that was to be the day on which I surrendered. I was commandeered in a cab to make sure I made the flight home; relief all around that I was now someone else's responsibility.

That sortie will always be remembered and revered but never commemorated.

He seemed to have the special ability of separating the what from the who, putting boundaries between behaviours and the person that lay beneath. He held no judgment for the former and an unshakeable belief in the latter. His share of suffering seemed to result in compassion; simple, crude and yet comforting. I was so happy when my eldest told me she was stalking him on social media, teasing him about giving her a cousin she could cosset. My daughter is repairing the divide that was not her doing, and she is wise enough to work on this with the most willing participant.

He was not always so generous, though. Being a latch-key kid did offer the gift of independence, but without supervision or accountability, it also allowed the unleashing of our very worst behaviour. There was the one time he chucked a hefty wooden coat hanger at me for the hell of it. My mother was relieved to hear that there was only a minor wound to my temple and that the window was intact. Yes, he was lucky that his aim was good that day. My only sanctuary from his constant harassment was the toilet, the only room that had the luxury of a lock. Even then, he would rattle it to the extent of the chain and have me cowering in the corner. The lock was lost when the house was repainted, and I was no match for his strength and persistence. I shocked both him and me when scissors were snatched, and I began sprinting towards him down the hallway, shrieking like a banshee and waiting for a chance to strike. "Fuck, she's lost it", was all I heard as he fled outside. It was an accurate assessment of the situation. Still, it took me a long time to understand what it was I had lost.

It may have all made sense if I had known about karma back then. I could have understood his behaviour as payback for breaking my sister's nose with the wonky tennis racket. I had hurled it at her when she had denied me the right to play with the good one. I was merely told by my mother not to do it again. And there was the time I broke a Coke bottle over her kneecap. I can't remember why or whether there was any punishment for my wrongdoing.

My sister told me once that if I continued to kill the ants in the driveway, the King Ant would come and take me away. Maybe that was her subtle attempt to summon the nature spirits to help her alleviate the scourge that was her little sister. For me, though, the prospect sounded like a pleasant escape, so it did not stop my slaughter. I am far too grown up now to believe in such rubbish. I know there is no King Ant. But I have lived long enough to know that the Queen's handmaidens take many forms.

My brother and I sat silently for a while, his mere presence a powerful support. Then he wandered away, closing the door to leave me alone with my father's fading body.

Love was there, just like the last time. It was so hard to describe. I tried once for my psych, telling him there were no boundaries, only brightness; that it was intangible and yet immense, nothing and yet everything, impalpable and yet pervasive. It gave off a feeling that was completely new to me; unassuming, unconditional, and unwavering. The psych's response was some scientific mumbo jumbo about the tricks our minds can play on us in moments of shock. When, after a few chardonnays one night, I plucked the courage to share this experience with my father, his response was just as underwhelming. "I'm glad you felt something", was all he said. Both my psych and father were well versed in the invalidation of the invisible. Contemplating my father's response when I regained sobriety, I realised how sad it was. There had been so much ancestral armour applied over the years, all of it to prevent the appreciation of pain and pleasure and to reinforce rigid independence. How hard the hammering must have been to remove the desire for or ability to feel spiritual sustenance.

Love and Death were never discussed around our family dinner table and not in any deep way by my friends. So, before mum passed, I had not had the chance to consider the relationship between these two powers. When I first walked into the house after mum had died, I could have sworn that Death had heralded Love's darkness. For the house was filled with longing, loss, and lamentation. Only when I had a chance to sit beside mum, did I realise that Death had also opened the door for Love's brightest light.

Here, with dad, Love brought no new instructions, just the confirmation of my purpose - "pass it on." I am glad that Love had not previously declared a deadline for the passing on to be completed. Otherwise, it would have decided long ago that I was a failure. I was doing a better job lately though. I had been daring enough to develop my definition of love and proclaim its applicability to politics and corporate life. I had read volumes on other people's visions of Love and researched its many faces. I authored articles extolling its essential nature and unmasking the misconceptions that mangle its true meaning. I had become adept at advocating for Love. So far, the results were a few followers, a couple of clapping hands emojis and a trickle of thumbs-up. The marketing strategy for my Love Manifesto was still on the to-do list.

Sitting with Love again, I was encouraged to consider that passing it on was not that simple. Love was numinous, and most of my actions to date had been driven by neediness. The awe I felt confirmed that achievement did not lie in advertising its existence but in a daily discipline of dedicated care. I was coming to realise that success was not to be found by shouting in front of a crowd but by permitting it to pass peacefully through me. Love was not seeking a voice but a vein.

I wondered why others didn't notice Love. Maybe they did but didn't feel compelled to mention it. I was egotistical to think I alone would be gifted this most sacred of sensations. I am no sage, prophet, saint, or Rinpoche. I am just a sister who too easily forgets that these people are also well-practised at imprisoning their emotional experiences.

dad's body grew colder and I was soon interrupted by the teams tasked with certification and interment. I tried to withhold my frustration but could only manage niceties through gritted teeth. I had not yet seen the signs of his spirit passing, but I knew mentioning such things would be like rubbing salt crystals into fresh, stinging wounds. My beliefs, while a balm to my grief, would only be seen by the others there as brutal. Why couldn't they just let him lay longer? Why couldn't they give more time for his spirit to sit in this space before travelling on? Why hadn't I been organised enough to have candles and incense ready to speed up his exit? Not that my sister would likely have let me light them anyway. Regardless, I would have felt better prepared if I had some by the bed. At least then, my intentions would be evident and internally validated.

While the workers made many superficial statements about respect, dad's corpse was treated just like a problem to be fixed, a challenge to be completed and a mess that must be cleaned away. There was no honouring of the hands that held us as children, no song for the shoulders that bore so much stress, and no ode to the eyes that sprang to life when he smiled.

A lifetime of beliefs was embodied here, and memories were embedded in every muscle. This sacred structure had hosted Hope, Hurt, Trust and Torment within its walls, and each had written their wisdom upon them. This body had been the source of financial security for our family. And it had also been an enemy; another machine, moaning from lack of maintenance and not easily mended. It had done its duty and met every extreme expectation; lugging lumber, standing for hours on cold cement; skin, hair and lungs smothered in sawdust. It was bruised and broken, and its cuts were callously bathed in metho. It was severely shaken on every truck trip for supplies and made to operate on little sleep. It was stuffed with food that should not go to waste and denied the delights of holidays. This body wore the brunt of the protestant work ethic and now could finally rest.

But I wondered where all that energy would go. Would it simply separate from the body, evaporate into the heavens to be captured in the clouds? Or would it await entombment and filter through the casket and into the cemetery's soil?

After one last stroke of gratitude through my father's grey and gelid hair, I followed my brother and sister out of the way. We could not participate in the process that came next. We were not that important. We only got to stand by as his body was shuttled away. The departure of the doctors and funeral directors was swiftly followed by the shuffling away of my sister and brother. There was no longer any reason for them to stay.

Chapter 4

I was left alone in the small, silent house. There was no sunrise yet to bring light to this darkness, or birdsong to remind me that I was surrounded by life. The emotional toil of the preceding hours left no energy to explore Love further or to search for dad's spirit. I had done the latter the night mum died, and was afforded the opportunity. But instead of enlightenment, it ended in embarrassment.

On the night of mum's death, I was laying in bed processing the presence in her room I had experienced and the message to "pass it on." Gradually, the aura in my room shifted from unremarkable to truly awesome—not like the hippy, hedonistic description, but in the sincere sense of wonderous. I had a feeling that this was an invitation, and so responded by asking mum to show me where she was. I wanted to see, and wanted to know. I felt myself lift from my body and I knew she was all too willing to grant this wish. Partly separated I started to panic. Fear forced me back, and I found myself apologising for my cowardice. Instead of securing my sense of self-worth, this shattered it. I called myself spiritual but was too scared to be anything more than shallow.

However, this recoil response was not new and it was not the first time I had denied myself the chance to find deeper meaning. As a teenager, I spent hours in this same room scouring through books on witchcraft, rote-learning rituals and scribing a list of spells. I had a collection of crystals, candles, a pendulum and tarot cards and used them regularly. I knew there was much more to this earth than I could see, and was determined to be a part of this greater existence. I felt it each day in the breath of the breeze, the touch of the trees, the firmness of the ground and the ferocity of our log fire. I saw it spread out across the space of the sky, and in the playfulness of the stray kittens. It was close, it was caring, and it was a great comfort.

So, one night, when I was around fourteen, I decided I had the strength to meet this magnificence. The ambient music was playing on the tape recorder, the spells were being whispered, and my mind was alert for any shifts suggesting the existence of the ethereal. It all ended abruptly when the spiritual soundtrack went screwy, then stopped; the play button snapped off, and the candle flickered wildly. I was not ready. Instead of opening further, I leapt up to put the light on, jumped back into bed and put my head under the blankets and chanted, "go away". The rest of the night was spent praying that my amateur attempt at divination had not called forth anything demonic. That night, the line between natural and the super sort would not be crossed. Instead, the event would be used to confirm my lack of worth as a witch and an excuse to pack away the pagan propaganda.

Apart from sitting with Love by my dead parents' bedsides, I had yet to make more forays into the fields beyond my sight. Still, I often see white feathers appear at the most perfect times and in the most unexpected places and it gives me heart to think they are a gift from some sort of guide. I have collected and honoured each one, only to have them whisked away by the wind or lost in the mess of my everyday life. They ask if a tree falls in the forest, but nobody hears, did it ever truly fall? Likewise, if a white feather fell at my feet but now cannot be found, did it ever truly exist? So many others would try and tell me it was only my excitable imagination. Still, I am old and bold enough to honour my beliefs. My feathers are no fantasy.

And yet, I am reluctant to reach out any further. I have used the distractions of my daily routines and responsibilities to deny myself the space and time for further quests. While there is a nagging desire to know what is, it is matched by a nervousness about what is not. The push and pull of providence are evenly matched, keeping me meandering around the middle with no determined direction. It is this same indecision that keeps Secret stuck.

I did seek wisdom once from a Buddhist monk. I described my experience at my mother's deathbed and asked for his explanation. He suggested what I felt was an angel, a higher order being, offering assistance to my mother during the difficult transition to the bardo. I know this was also standing beside my father last night and was what I felt flowing downwards in his room. If this is the case, and angels were present for my parents at the time of their death, then what does this mean for me? Where was my mentor all those many years ago when my childhood ceased?

The slip into self-pity was distracted by the first-morning call of the crows. I had never taken the time before now to listen closely to them, but today they provided a much-needed diversion. I had read that the crows have a language all their own, but despite my longing, I could not understand what it was they were shouting across the sky. Was it merely a status update about how many of their murder were left standing after the nightly onslaught of snakes and feral cats? Perhaps each deep guttural sound offered gratitude for seeing this day's dawn. Maybe they were sharing meteorological musings and making plans around their predictions. It was not my privilege to know what their noises meant, but I thanked them anyway for their presence.

As the first light of the morning leaked across the sky, the base notes of these bigger birds were joined by the top notes of the tiny ones. Their high-pitch whistles were a stochastic conversation, sometimes promising predictability and then tossing in a little surprise. The kookaburras came next, their cackle convincing the community around them to prepare for powerful storms. I love to watch as they line the fences of my home, waiting, waiting, waiting, and then, like lightning, darting down to grab an unsuspecting lizard. I find their speed and accuracy are amazing, but I suspect these skills are believed awful by their prey. Sometimes, one, who I like to call Spike (because of its punk-style strip of hair) comes and sits on my front deck. My little dog and I spy on it through the blinds, admiring the blue sheen of its wings, the solid strength of its torso, and the blade-like precision of its beak.

And there it was, the melodic mayhem of the cockatoo. While the chuckle of Kookaburras always made me smile, it was nothing compared to the internal celebration that came with the cockatoo's screech. Their voice was not pretty and would not even be categorised as pleasant; but I found it so powerful. The cockatoo never cared about the insult that its individuality may bring. It lets it out loudly, seemingly unphased by other's opinions. Back home, they hang out at the mandarin tree that bridges over my neighbour's boundary. They find the fruit, peel away the skin and scatter it over my lawn. It makes a delightful orange decoration on an otherwise drab landscape. It is not lost on me that this avian wonder is also the source of the white feathers, which I have come to associate with wisdom. As such, their presence is always welcome.

As the sky brightened further, the activity in the natural world was soon matched by the music of man-made machines. A hum came from the highway and there was a regular scrape and crunch of wheels rolling over gravel. These mundane messengers made it clear that it was time to tell my daughters that dad had died.

The girls were distraught with the news that they had lost their treasured grandfather, and the last remaining link to this side of their lineage. They had been born well after the death of their Nan, and so had not known her, a source of great sadness for all of us. They would get some sense of what they had missed in the hugs from their other grandmother, but they would never fully understand the extent of doting they would have received. Mum's generosity knew no bounds. She would have had a fantastic time trying to fatten them with festive treats and delighting them with new dresses. Their beds would have been made beautifully with layers of luxurious toppers and soft sheets. She would have welcomed them with warm hugs that never wore off.

Now, though, there was not much to be said. Space was created for silence between the shedding of tears. I arranged for them to arrive in two days, just in time for the funeral. This would also allow me to work through my feelings so I could help them care for theirs.

I met my brother and sister at the funeral home, and an hour was spent understanding the activities occurring behind the doors and the events of the next few days. We were all given duties, partially to help us feel a part of the process, but also I surmised to distract us from our distress. My brother was to organise the pall bearers, sourcing those of strong body and mind, and with sufficient respect for this weighty responsibility. My sister, being the eldest, was to oversee the eulogy, with all agreeing that, given the emotion of the occasion, its delivery may best be delegated. I was tasked with selecting the readings, finding the readers and preparing the printed program. There was a great benefit in the busyness of these burdens and cleverness in forcing a connection with those who care. I did not have to look at my sister to know that despite her grief, her guard was still up, and I wondered if those walls ever did come down.

I re-entered the cottage exhausted but managed to make a few easy decisions and quick phone calls. I fielded a few from friends and neighbours, expressing their condolences and checking if there was anything we needed. I had someone bring me cake, coming over only when they saw the car in the yard, and some flowers arrived that, after being met with muted thanks, served as a fitting tribute beside the death bed.

As the day began to close, the distant thunder presented a provocation, poking and prodding. Passivity was replaced with an intense irritation, which could not be washed away with toast and tea. As the sounds became more ominous, my annoyance was pushed into outrage. And with one loud boom, all the Anger I had never been allowed to feel before burst forth. I was captured by a terrific tempest. It twisted time and thrust me forward into the funeral. There I was watching my cousin as he leant over dad's coffin to pay his respects.

This hypocrisy only encouraged my hostility. My cousin did not care when he lured dad's daughter into indecency and cursed dad's child with such a cruel secret. In my vision he was putting on a show of his sadness, bowing to my father's body and holding his own heart. This made the bile brew in my breast and bitterness burst forward.

I was surprised by the severity and endlessness of my seething, for it was a force I had never felt before. I was sure that if my cousin was in front of me right now, and could choose my weapons, I would splash acid in his face then proceed to stab him repeatedly until he was ripped apart. Even this would not be sufficient revenge.

This hate was bringing with it heat. My chest felt like it was on fire, but I was no longer afraid of this furnace or of allowing it freedom. I let it loose, and it flowed upwards and outwards. My heart was pumping hard, my arms primed for punching, my eyes were ready to emit evil, and my voice was set to spit venom. I pilfered through the pile of papers beside dad's phone and found the address book, adding my cousin to the contact list on my phone, assuring myself that I would use this soon, but that I had to be strategic in my reprisal.

As the water welled into puddles outside, became obsessed. Bed was just another place for plotting the inevitable encounter. I set the scene in my mind and worked through successive scenarios, mentally noting how each scored on the sinister scale. I worked through a multitude of options, preparing pros and cons, challenges and contingencies. I built a roadmap of revenge and, around midnight was finally ready to avenge my father for an act he knew nothing about. Despite a little voice telling me this was ludicrous, Anger was adamant that my cousin needed to pay. Its confidence was comforting, and I willingly conceded.

Because how could I be allowed to hurt this much, and my cousin get off scot-free? Why should he get to parade around as a moral, mighty man, while I end up as a damaged and depreciated daughter? How can he get away with being seen as the respectful one while I end up denigrated as deranged?

There must be justice, a righting of wrongs. And I was adamant that on this night, with the help of the thunder and lightning, I would find the words that would reverse the roles of sinner and saint, victor and victim. I knew some great-hearted guides were telling me to forget this folly and to follow the path of forgiveness. I could hear all my self-help heroes telling me my concern should be caring for my children instead of concocting callous vengeance. There were gurus calling on me to choose acceptance and compassion over certainty and closure. Anger assured me that if they could truly appreciate my reality, they would also advise the actions of acrimony. Their idealism was born of ignorance, and their lack of knowledge made them naïve. They suggested spiritual theories rather than practical solutions when it was clear that the only way out was through confrontation.

I was stringing together snippets of spite to make an opening sentence when things came unstuck. "I know what you did", sounded like a suitable start to my strike, but it was untrue. I could not feign a false confidence that I knew the facts. Starting my speech with "I remember", was setting myself up for my memory to be contested. Trying something like "your actions caused so much pain", only opened the door for him to profess his own. He may seek to compete and match my misery with his own. I may be forced to feel his own father wounds and consider that blame lay beyond us both. But his father was no longer around to field the fault. And he is an adult now and needs to take full responsibility for the trauma he has wrought.

It could have been the tiredness creating such irrationality, but the at the time, the logic felt sound. I had to confront my cousin. And to do this I had to have all the facts. So, I must find someone who is all-seeing. I needed someone strong enough to push Memory aside and haul Secret into the light. I need someone with the power to shake Secret until all the truths fall out on the floor, but also compassionate enough to sit with me while I map the trail of trauma. I needed someone wise enough to help me write the words that will break the bastard and give him some of my Shame and yet someone gentle enough to then guide me through my grief. Someone who will force away Fear and lift me out of this hell I have created.

I had to call Angel forward.

Yes, Angel, I am ready.

Chapter 5

The storm kit was easy to find. It was wedged in the well-stocked pantry alongside other supplies dad considered essential, such as sugar, salt, brown sauce, baked beans and butter cake mix. It was packed in my sister's old school port. The dark brown vinyl had deteriorated over the forty years since its use, and would have been considered ugly by today's standards. Still, it was not here for its beauty but for its utility. Nothing was ever thrown away in our house that could be used, repaired or gifted to someone who could use or repair it themselves. I am sure dad considered me lazy or selfish, or both, when he saw the pile I placed on the curb for council pick-up. Perhaps he lamented that his legacy of caring for the artefacts of our lives had been lost. My parents' hard work meant I did not know lack, and maybe this had made me careless.

Seeing my sister's, I wondered where my old school bag was. I did love that little yellow box with the shiny silver locks. Carrying it made me feel so very important. It was sturdy too, allowing me to stand on it and making the shape of a star. I remember adorning the inside with KISS stickers, and being fascinated with the musician's costumes and makeup. There was something so alluring about the idea that I could cover my face with colour and then be free to act, entertain and attract. My port was probably stashed in the shed at my childhood home, now a safe haven for spiders. Or, it had been thrown into landfill long ago, my sister not deeming it worthy of retention. Yet its Memory still held an energy that created a sense of excitement for me now and one that fed into this next foray.

Inside this poor old port were torches, batteries, candles and matches, all dusty from disuse. For the past few years, dad would have used any blackout as a sign to go to bed. There were no children or pets to care for anymore and no work others were waiting for. He was free to enjoy watching the war of the weather and wait for it to drift away.

I stopped briefly to consider the stupidity of lighting the space. Surely, the supernatural creature I was looking for could conjure their own radiance. I smiled as I realised these candles were not for Angel but for me. They were a simple example of the illumination I was seeking and an item that clearly captured my intention. Besides, in every spiritual practice I had pursued over the years, candles always held a special place. It seemed a universal symbol for all those seeking the light. It's just that the light had many different names.

The candles were placed in safe positions around my bed. While I had imagined images of this place inflamed, and I found some solace in these sentiments, I knew the reality would only wreak more havoc. The first light from each candle was like a flare, expressing its fury about being forgotten for so long. When the flickering ceased, the flame stood still, sharing a great sense of strength.

Beside one candle, I placed the incense I had brought with me from home but had not yet dared to use out of concern for my sister's judgement. The scent was so different from the one swayed around during church services, yet it felt so much more familiar. I often wondered whether my fondness for yoga, Buddhism, lentils and sandalwood were indicators of previous lives spent on the subcontinent.

I sat on the bed and joined my palms together in the position of prayer. Perhaps this was merely a habit and a superficial symbol, but it seemed proper given the solemnity of the situation. Over the years, I have repeated this same process a thousand times. It had either ended in resignation, resolve, or meandered into meditation. But tonight, I did something I had never before had the foresight to do.

I asked.

I asked to meet Angel.

I can't remember the words I used, and I would be loath to list them, lest they be lauded as a spell and sold to subscribers of a second-rate spiritual site.

But with my begging, Angel began.

It was born of the white wisps rising from the incense. I watched, enchanted by the gentle, silent, swirling strands, the see-through ribbon rolling and rippling. The haze had some humour, playing purposefully as it began to push forward and portray a full human figure. It was such a serene process, such a delicate dance. It allowed space at each stage, sought my permission, and allowed me to pause progress at any time. This creation was done with such care that it piqued my curiosity, not challenged my comfort. This was not the sinister swirling of storm clouds that always wrought worry but the patient, slow-shifting shapes I saw in the sky as a child.

There was a rhythm, though, by which Angel was revealed, a pulse from which it was produced. It was built from the boots, the smoke clearing to show strapped sandals with a metallic sheen. The pants appeared as a blend of black and brown, woolly and worn. The knees were protected with armour plates, pleated to allow prostrations. A cape was draped across the thighs, beginning with burnt umber and progressing to a brilliant sunset orange. His hands were sturdy yet smooth, the palms facing outwards, projecting peace. The belt was basic, and the buckle beautiful in its simplicity. The shirt flowed forth, a muted blue, its arms adorned with armour. On each side, the wings grew wide. They were of brown earth and built like a bird of prey, capable of powerful pursuit, prolonged exploration and sustained protection. At this moment though, they were perched behind the body purposefully. The hair spread forth from the shoulders, shifting between hues of bronze, copper and gold. The jugular notch was unguarded, and the neck was noble. His features became clear and were delicate and well-balanced. His eyes were of the sky, with the azure aura of a clear day. The smoke had sewn together a full shape, and the transparent had turned into something I could now touch. And now finally saw a face that was all too familiar.

It was the same angel I had a photo of in an unused Filofax back home. I had seen this image in a painting on my first trip to Florence; drawn to this character while wandering the halls of the Academia and inexplicably enchanted by him. Even the marvels of Michealangelo could not compete with the connection I felt with this composition. I came to know Angel first when he was kneeling in the corner of a much more significant scene, but this was lost when I cut him from it and saved his solo figure. I have no knowledge of the work that was Angel's world, nor the artist that created him. To this day, I am still unsure whether it was the artist's gift that drew my attention to Angel or my own desire to find a target for affection.

Regardless of the reason, Angel has been with me ever since. He used to travel with me everywhere, folded into my diary. Now, he is planted somewhere at the back of my cupboard. I had not seen him in years but my thoughts of him were still as tender as our first meeting. This angel could have taken any shape. How wise it was to have chosen one which already held so much admiration.

Angel was dressed like a soldier, and I sensed he had seen many battles. He had put his life on the line for a prophecy, philosophy, person or place. Yes, this angel had fought for others, but I felt he had also warred with demons that were purely his own. He stood now as a peacekeeper, embodying the Love I had experienced, but which issued forth more subtly.

I noticed that Angel wore no jewellery, no trinkets telling of allegiance to another. His fingers held no evidence of idolatry, his wrists were absent from worship, and his neck naked from displays of adoration. This bareness brandished a lack of bias and made me believe I may be treated honourably. Out of habit, I had to examine his eyebrows. They were just like mine, an inner tuft trailing into the invisible. I wondered whether he had been kind enough to manifest these for my comfort or whether this was a sign that he had once shared the same wounds.

Anger was humbled by the heavenly, shrinking into the shadows. I sat. Angel stood. Both in silence. The swirling space between us settled into stillness, and we began to take our first few breaths together. There was no rush in this need for mutual regard. Our eyes embraced, erupting tears in mine; brushing them away broke the sense of abeyance, and I felt compelled to act. I was unsure if he could read my thoughts, so I decided to speak.

"Thank you for coming. "

A small nod and a slight smile provided acknowledgement.

"May I know your name?"

"I go by many. What name would be meaningful for you?"

"I have known you as Angel for many years."

With a generous and genuine simper, he said, "I am Angel."

This statement sat between the strong and the serene, the confident and the calm and convinced me he was capable of a broad scope of expression.

"Can I ask you some questions?"

"Of course, Juno."

I was relieved he used my name and did not do the "sweetheart" or "darling" thing. I would have considered this an act of condescension and a cause to reduce his credibility. With my name, I had no doubt he knew who I was and that I was not just some generalisation seeking guidance.

"Can you please tell me what happened with my cousin, here, in this room when I was a child? I need to know the exact details so that I can decide what to do next."

"Juno, I cannot tell of things that are not clear for you."

"But why?"

"I must abide by your own powers of self-protection."

"Were you here, Angel?"

"Yes."

"You saw what happened?"

"Yes."

"So, you were a witness to my abuse."

"Yes."

"Please, the uncertainty is driving me crazy. I don't understand. Why can't you tell me what you saw?"

"I cannot interfere with your truth."

"But what if I can't trust my truth?"

Angel did not respond. There was no need. The answer was obvious.

"Angel, why didn't you intervene?"

"I have no power over a person's will."

"Well, then will you help me deliver some justice?"

"What additional compensation do you seek? If you hope to hurt someone or something then I cannot help. I cannot harm another."

"But why should my cousin be able to get away with the corruption of a child?"

"Juno, all of the consequences of his actions are not clear to you, but I can assure you that he has created a legacy that will last longer than this lifetime."

I realised that this message was meant to relieve my need for retribution and remind me of my personal responsibility.

"Then will you take me to the Akashic records so that I can find my own answers."

"Juno, there is no purely objective source of information for a person's life. Every book inherently holds some bias. And every story holds some residue of the speaker."

The use of my name, which I once found reassuring, was becoming annoying, almost taunting.

"Still, I wouldn't mind another opinion."

"Those are already available to you."

The fondness that once felt so firm was now being fettered away by Frustration. Interestingly, my irritation seemed to increase Angel's illumination. Or perhaps it was Anger's ire, emboldened by the evasive answers, that was growing his glare.

"So, you have nothing for me?"

At this stage, I was averse to calling him Angel.

"You were meant to protect me from harm, but you didn't. You are meant to help me resolve my problems, but you refuse. I'm sorry, but what is it you do exactly?"

I shocked myself with how quickly I slipped into sarcasm and disappointed myself when I denied him the chance to defend himself.

"Do you know how much pain this has caused?"

"Yes."

"And yet you won't help."

"Juno, I cannot help in the way you want. I cannot work against your own wisdom, nor pare back your self-protection. I cannot inspire you to investigate the insights that are awaiting you. I cannot turn reality into fantasy, repair the sins of the past and erase your pain. I will not bend the path that may lead to brilliance, nor nullify the numinous."

"But Angel, what you see as wisdom is actually a weakness."

"That is your opinion."

"So, all I am hearing is what you cannot do. Angel, what can you do for me?"

The begging belied the brutality from which the words were born.

"Juno, you will only get the answers you seek when you start asking the right questions. The solutions that will bring peace require contemplation grounded in compassion."

I could sense that Frustration had also begun to infect his faith. Patience was becoming progressively more problematic.

"Juno, the roles you require of me are of your own making. They are neither righteous nor responsible. I must go for my presence here is no longer productive."

I was suddenly sad that I had allowed my bitterness to obstruct this opportunity and that I had allowed Anger to crawl out of the corner.

"I am sorry, Angel," I said through streaming tears. For one who had spent so much of their life emotionally repressed, this was a revolution.

"Will you come back again if I ask?"

"Yes, Juno, I will. But know that I am always around you."

"Why haven't I seen you before now?"

"You have, but did not recognise me. Our eyes meet in the creatures you see every day, and I am always delivering reminders that I am here, thinking of you, and waiting for your call. Sometimes you find the tokens, and these are now the treasures placed on your mantle. Most days though you are too preoccupied with your own pursuits to perceive me."

"I'm sorry, Angel. I don't mean to ignore you. I get so confused. This pain just seems to consume me. Is there any further guidance you can give to help me find clarity?"

"Yes, Juno. I can leave you with these questions. Who would you be without this pain? And who can you be with it?"

He stepped forward and knelt on one knee, the armour clinking against the carpet. He looked into my eyes and held my hand, and at that moment, I felt the grasp of Grace.

Angel stood slowly and then dissolved, flesh and cloth turning to mist.

With Angel's absence, all I could feel was fatigue. There was no fuel left to debrief, only enough energy to extinguish the candles and collapse into bed. My girls would be here tomorrow, and I had to restore my strength to help them through their suffering.

Chapter 6

Grief had joined the girls on their journey, walked off the plane with them, and stood beside us as we held each other. In the past, airports had been a place of adventure, exuding excitement of explorations to come and pleasures from retail purchases. However the purpose of this trip held no such delights. It was a sombre one and it was honoured through cuddles and concerned faces. Tears, though, would be kept for the cottage. Memory was marking this time uniquely for each girl, but I knew well the many layers of sadness it was setting down.

We were all unsure how long my mother would stay alive, and so it was decided at the time it would be be best for me to return to Brisbane and to work, with plans made for me to come back within a few weeks. Getting off the plane after leaving my mother, I was overcome by a complex plaiting of emotions. I was troubled with the extent of her suffering, knowing she was negotiating with Death on the other side of the door. I was sitting with the desperate thought that I may never return to her; there would be no longer the harbourage I once called home. And there was the intense sorrow imagining the children yet to come, growing up without the indulgences of their grandmother. Shame was there too, telling me I should not have left her side, that I was selfish for following her instruction, that she really did want me to stay, and that I knew it all along. Adding to all of this was the hurt in my husband's eyes when I could not display the happiness he expected upon seeing him. I am sure he thought he could actually console me, but could not tell whether this belief was borne from childishness or conceit.

With the girls loaded into the car, we had the same drive ahead that I endured the day mum died. Even after frantically booking last-minute flights, I had arrived too late, getting the call on the way to the airport that she had gone. This drive then, this one my girls were also about to go through, was like a passage between two places, allowing some space for preparation but never enough time for a full transition. I remember being chauffeured by my maternal cousin to my mourning family but spending this journey delighting in the expanse and brightness of the sky. I was not disturbed by the thought I shared only with my mother; that it was a truly beautiful day to die. The weather at dad's passing was just as dramatic, just at the other extreme of the spectrum.

Today, the girls would be accompanied by commanding clouds and patient peeks of the sun. They were making their own meanings from nature's messages and choosing the scenes to help them make sense of their sadness. I had parked my experience with Angel in my personal space so I could be present for the girls, awaiting the time in which it could be fully appreciated.

We delayed the inevitable arrival into dad's absence with a daughter's disconsolate duties, filling in time between the printers and the priest by camping at a café. Such an outing would usually feel like such a treat, but today, it was an effort. Rushing to the display cabinet was replaced with resigned responses of "whatever", and there was no magic to be found in this menu. Pastries that would have created so much delight and shared experiences were partitioned and picked at in silence. Drinks that would have been moved around the table for all to taste were now held tight and sipped thoughtlessly. I knew that Grief would mute and muffle our pleasures for some time to come, and would be a constant companion for my girls. It would stay with them, merely dwindling in significance across the years, maybe one day shrinking enough so that they can climb around it. Someday, it would become a small stone in their shoe, but for now, Grief was global and gigantic.

We headed to the church to meet the priest who would do the service. He may have been a faithful father to some, but to me, he was simply a stranger. He wanted to know about dad and his faith; what kind of person he was so he could prime his speech. The fact that I had to provide this information should have been some signal that dad held his convictions close to his chest. My father did not confide in anyone, not even his wife or children, and he certainly would not have been counselled by a man of the cloth. Worries were signs that your strength was flawed, and he would not want to flaunt this to anyone. Yet, I described a man who, despite his own sometimes idiotic independence, gave generously. Even when his body was bearing down upon him, he found the energy to help friends and neighbours. In his darkest days, it was not his own demise that brought him down but the frustration that came with being unable to attend to others. This image invoked an insight; perhaps dad gave to others what he was desperately wanting for himself. Was his charity a kind of transference?

Despite my dad being such a decent human being, it was never enough for his brother-in-law, a born-again Christian, who had condemned my father to damnation many years before. This man, my Uncle, was confident to his core that heaven was reserved solely for followers of Jesus. In a heated conversation over a kitchen bench, I confirmed his belief that, despite dad's dedication to goodness, he would still be whisked to hell because he did not pay homage to God's heir. It was a debate that, while decades past, still had the ability to infuriate me. Surely, years of selflessness would count for something in a God concerned with teaching compassion. Or maybe this was just another chink in the chain of hypocrisy that girded the Church. I dared not seek any solace from the priest. There was the chance that this man was adept at the same style of judgement, and my girls did not need any more trauma.

I left as soon as I felt assured that the priest sensed my father's specialness. Then we went up the path to visit mum's grave. It was far too long since I had been there and I momentarily forgot where to find it. Shame stared at me with a smirk on his face until I secured the spot. Then the girls and I stood before the humble headstone with the fantastic floral tribute. I remembered then how much mum's site was cared for by others; her sisters were dedicated to celebrating her life through this cenotaph. In contrast, my offerings had been paltry and sporadic.

A realisation made my heart fall away. Mum's sisters were ageing too, tired and tormented by increasing limitations, their worlds becoming smaller through weariness and worn-out parts. And I was certainly no consistent contributor, providing some fabric flowers every few years. I would not blame anyone if they assumed that I had forgotten her. I could not stay there any longer with Shame lingering and spoiling the sentiments.

On the way back to the cottage I created a diversion by stopping in to see my brother. He was in his workshop, gloomy and grease ridden. He was well-trained in distracting from difficult emotions. We all did the same after mum's death, conveniently choosing our individual commitments over sharing our sympathies and supporting each other's loss. We weren't used to leaning on each other, and even having our mother ripped from us would not make us take that leap. We found our own ways to fuddle through the loss, forming adaptations of anxiety, atheism and alcoholism along the way.

The hugs from my brother were cautious this time, conserved to prevent a possible outburst. There were also far fewer words than usual. He asked if we were ok, to which each of us nodded assent with ashen faces. "And you?, was met with a "yes". He confirmed that he did not need anything and that we would meet later at the funeral home.

Entering the cottage with the girls was eerie. They had only ever known this place with their Poppy waiting inside, usually with a homemade cake covered in thick, sweet icing and a hot chocolate crowned by whipped cream and sprinkles. Poppy's snacks came with a special aura that I could never replicate. Perhaps our absence had made his heart grow fonder, so much so that it flooded into his food.

As I had expected, seeing the space in which Poppy once sat brought tears. We cuddled on the sofa beside his chair and cried. Words were whispered between the weeping. Sobs were like stabs of reality, recognising that Poppy would never be here to greet us again. There would be no more mountainous meals, presents of cash through the post, or Sunday night phone calls. There would be no more trips out to his property, and jaunting around on the back of his Ute to chase his cows. No longer would there be competitions to choose a name for the newest calf. The girls would miss so much.

With dad's passing also went the tension of withholding Secret and the intermittent temptations to show it to him in all its obscure disgrace. However, I was far from free. Now I was shrouded in an itchy and irritating robe of regret, remorse and self-reproach and this suit sat firmly and solely on my shoulders.

When the last wild wave of anguish washed ashore, and we were all spent from sadness, we had a difficult discussion about sleeping arrangements. There were only two options: sleeping in Secret's room, with one girl on the single bed and another on a mattress, or the bed where Poppy had taken his last breath. Predictably, they chose the former. I hesitated to put the girls in that room, thinking I could move the bedding to the lounge. But it had been purified somewhat after Angel's presence and its bitter energy balanced by his benevolence.

I was left with the site where dad had finally succumbed to what he believed would be an endless sleep. I knew that others may think me disrespectful or even disgusting, but I knew this space as Divine. Perhaps it was to placate my daughter's pain or provide myself with the promise of peace, but I told them of how Love had been here, guiding Poppy the same way it had helped Nan. I hoped they may know it directly one day, and not in the diluted form of my insufficient interpretation.

We were preparing the beds when my Aunty arrived. She was so much older than dad but always looked years younger. I had remembered her as being rotund, a quality that came with a sense of relief. For here was a woman overweight and well, heavy and happy. For me, her figure was filled with hope. The Aunty that crossed the threshold now, though, was so much thinner. Dad had told me each week of her persistent health problems, and it was clear that they had eaten away at any excess energy. Her face was, as always, free from makeup but covered in kindness. How could I possibly destroy her dignity with my story of her son's sins?

She was followed in by her daughter, the sister of the suspect, and the cousin, whom in my version of events, I had credited with ceasing the persecution. But there was no relationship or regard that one would expect between refugee and rescuer. A quick hello was followed by casual chit-chat about how long it had been since our last meeting. We landed on the likelihood that it had been a few decades, at which point she handed over a cake and went across the road to see my sister.

My Aunt took a foil-covered casserole dish to the bench and inspected her grand-nieces. I made tea and we all sat and ate cake while the girls answered easy questions such as their age, year, favourite subject, sport, and pets. Their lives were largely unknown past Poppy's perimeter. The friendly foray was forced back into Grief's field with Aunty's proclamation that, "Poppy was so proud of you," and then went ahead to point to all the evidence. There were photos of the pair plastered across the fridge. Every school photo I had ever sent to dad was stacked in sequence on the bookshelf. The mugs the girls painted for him one bitter winter's day were dusty but still displayed.

I tried to disguise my ignorance about her own lineage by inquiring after her own grandchildren. Beyond her daughter, I was dumb to her descendants. She proudly declared she was a great-grandmother three times over and showed us on her phone the photos of the people we would see tomorrow. I felt so fondly for her but thought it presumptuous that we would seek out strangers during our distress. Her daughter returned, signalling it was time to depart. Arising, Aunty announced there was a lovely lamb casserole on the bench for tea. I saw my daughter's eyes enlarge and the word lamb, and I did not have the heart to tell her I was a vegetarian. My mind meandered to the baby sheep they suckled at the school fairs, and I had to suppress my distaste. Still, I knew how much it meant to this woman to give, and so I thanked her genuinely for her generosity. On parting, she confirmed that we would meet again in a few hours at the funeral home, and this thought came with an excruciating cramp.

Cleaning up from afternoon tea, the ache continued, causing me to contemplate the confusing combination of the words funeral and home. Any home I had ever known had been a base where one began, from which one could go beyond, and to which one could always come back. The house we would enter tonight was one for which there was no return, where there was a going out but no coming back.

This situation sounded like the circumstance around my childhood home. I wondered if I would ever return to it or whether it would remain simply as a house I passed by on the way down to the petrol station, and, like a tour guide, presented to my children from afar as the place I grew up.

I did discuss with the girls what we were to do next, but nothing would prepare them for seeing their first dead body. Before we got out of the car, I made sure they knew there was no expectation to join me at the coffin. I told them that an open casket can be confronting, so they only needed to come if they felt comfortable. I almost said, "or curious," but I felt this comment may be taken as macabre. Yet I wanted to know what dad's body looked like without its life force. I had easily aligned to the Buddhist beliefs that to ignore the inevitable was the height of idiocy. While I was not racing to contemplate my conclusion at charnel grounds, I would take each chance to allow familiarity to deflate fear.

Every experience I had to date with a dead body had convinced me of the magnificence of the human form with which we were gifted and how it was constructed to be the conduit between heaven and earth. It also ensured me that this is not where we would be entombed for eternity. The energy that once excited this object had well and truly exited and existed elsewhere. The intimacy that came with being beside the immortal was precious, and the chance to send thanks for all that this human body had given was humbling.

However, I was also well aware that I had never been forced to view a body that had met its end through violence.

Inside was a small gathering, preparing to say their private goodbyes before the public parade the next day. I thought about whether these people saw this event as a moment to treasure or more like mandatory torture. We were greeted by the director and shown to the spaces that held seats and refreshments, the latter providing a convenient distraction from the room ahead. There was some mingling, muted conversations, embraces and tears. The awkwardness was magnified by the meeting between cousins. The children that cuddled years ago had become almost unrecognisable to each other. No one had the strength to muster small talk, so we simply sat, sipped some cold cordial and waited for our turn to enter the tomb.

I tried desperately not to corrupt this cherished occasion by seeking out the accused, believing that to bring my scars into this sanctuary would be sacrilege. But Angel's words about the wisdom that my wounds held kept ringing within. At that moment, I realised that I had spent my life punishing myself for my weakness, while both my head and heart deserved some respect. I had treated them with so much scorn, and yet, despite my best attempts at self-destruction, they had sustained me thus far. Perhaps it was time to explore another path. So, right then, I vowed to no longer admonish any experience, either arising from external sources or internal conflict. Nor would I reject the personal protectors who rose to the challenge when I needed support. Yes, now they may be seen as problematic, but then, they were my best attempt to stay alive and somewhat sane. The amnesia, the anorexia, the alcoholism and need to be alone were all adaptations, and must be respected as such. It was remarkable how empowering this shift in perspective was. I had switched from being fragile and faulty to a master at making it through. However, this triumph was not to be tested on this night, with my cousin not coming to this compound. But I was sure its strength would be strained in the following days.

When the director signalled that our turn had come, my questions to the girls were met with nods of assent. I held their hands, and we headed towards the casket.

The sense of peace I felt in my earlier experiences with the deceased was still present as I stood beside dad. Something about the stillness and silence of the shape helped me believe that somewhere, dad's spirit was also at rest. I lay my hand on his forehead and said, "I love you, Dad, and thank you for all you have given us." It may have seemed like a last-ditch, desperate dedication. Still, I was reassured, knowing it was a repetition of the conversations shared every Sunday and reinforced in the last few days of his life. I was prepared for my girls to be freaked out and wanting to flee. But instead of fright, there was flow. My eldest touched his hand. There was a moment of recoil when she met the extreme chill of the skin, but she replaced it after an instant of introspection. It was certainly the part of a corpse I found the most curious. Nothing can prepare you for how cold our bodies become when there is no more warmth of the will or heat from the heart. Of course, the chill of dad's body now was very much man-made and aimed at preventing the putrefaction that would be perceived as unpleasant. Mother

Earth and her subsurface society would be the only ones bearing witness to its withering.

My youngest followed my example and put her hand on dad's forehead. She held steady, but her eyes showed a second of shock. Love was there, landing lightly over us, and I knew dad would be proud of this legacy. I was swept back twenty years to the same meeting we had to send off my mother. I had no children to care for back then and could crumple into my own concerns. With my girls by my side, the process felt much more expansive; like I was given a great honour to help them through this rite of passage.

When I felt the time was right, we returned and took our place. Seats that meant nothing to us at the start were now cherished friends. When the procession had been completed and the last cuddles concluded, we confirmed arrangements for the next day and dispersed. There was no discussion about a group gathering or the sharing of a supper. We were all left to wander our own way through the evening.

In contrast to the convulsions and cries of earlier hours, the car was now a capsule of the catatonic. No one was hungry, but I was compelled by my parental commission to provide food. The thought of broiled baby animals was too much to bear, so I headed to the nearest Chinese takeaway and grabbed a small family banquet.

While waiting to be provided with a plethora of plastic bags secured from spillage with double knots, I remembered standing in the same place as a child. We were compensated for attending church on Saturday nights with Chinese takeaway afterwards. There was never any discussion about the cuisine or alternatives advanced. At that time there was only Chinese or Lebanese takeaway available in town, and my parents would not try the latter. I never did understand the reluctance to explore something different, but the negative responses to my queries made it obviously non-negotiable.

Mum would always get chicken and almonds, and dad, curry steak. Mum would always spend the night scraping small splinters of nuts off her false teeth. Dad would always spend the night irate at the indigestion that surely succeeded spicy food. I can't remember what menu options were offered to the children. Still, it would not have included any suspicious seafood or horrible bottom-feeders. Likely it would have been something battered and sweetened. There was always fried rice; the only time our house held a grain that wasn't ground down, bleached and baked into bread. It would last for days as leftovers, the little green peas getting wrinkly, the ham hard and the rice dry, but nothing that could not be made edible by smothering over with some tomato sauce.

Back at the cottage, I unloaded our haul. There were crunchy spring rolls, prawn chips that popped on your tongue, sticky honey dishes and fragrant rice. Its appearance and aromas lifted our mood but could do little to stir our appetites. There was a tiny thrill when my eldest reached for the fortune cookies, for then I knew that Grief could not constrain every curiosity. There was something so compelling about the crack of the opening and the sound of the message sliding outwards, embraced to the end by the shell. Heeding my daughter's heroism the rest of us actioned our own cookie adventures.

As per our family custom, the small white strips were laid on the table for all to view. I gave voice to the missives; reading them out loud seemed to make them real.

"A person that values its privileges above its principles soon loses both."

"We leave our fingerprints on the lives of those we have touched."

"The best way to find the right answer is to ask the right question."

I could not restrain the smile, thinking of how Angel may have played a hand in this dispatch. I had stopped believing in coincidence long ago, finding the idea of serendipitous signals much more reassuring. However, as Angel rightly identified, I was only sometimes open to receiving them. I was just sorry we never had the enjoyment of exploring fortune cookie communications when I was a child and encouraged to consider that they came to us from something more meaningful than chance.

It was only 8pm when we were all tucked into the beds that would bear our burdens. My eldest's toes hung over the edge of the blow-up mattress, but she was too tired to afford them any attention. I had removed the orange bedspread from where my youngest lay, unable to assuage the anxiety attached to her being wrapped in such torment. I lay in bed where Love had lived so strongly, wishing the impossible for my girls, that tonight they would find some peace. They each had their earphones in, so at least they had a place to escape.

Sinking into the mattress, I considered where dad's energy may have gone. The room felt so different from the day of his death, but what was the cause of the deviation? Was the energy still there, but was my pain preventing its perception? Or had it travelled somewhere else, a destiny I could not comprehend. Perhaps it had magically transformed into something more mundane. Had it split and settled within the items around the room? Had it drifted and embedded itself within the garden that he doted upon? Maybe others sensed these things, and this was the source of their sentimentality; their clinging to and caring for artefacts. Sometimes, I wished for the ability to cherish such things, feeling faulty for my inability to attach myself to inanimate objects. But from my time with Buddhism I was well versed in the Law of Impermanence. I knew that these things would one day break and leave me. It made sense to me then to prevent any future pain, it was best to remain dispassionate.

With this reflection, I realised my own duplicity. While I would not dedicate myself to things that would disappear, I was committed to clinging to pain from the past, not permitting it to simply pass. While I had a distaste for tangible tokens of times past, I had allowed one event to embed itself within every cell and its design to define me. While I could easily dismiss so much sadness as assumed, I had set out to make sure this suffering had a safe home in my head and in my heart. All I had ever known was myself as the girl with the secret, as one who had been abused. Despite every other achievement, I routinely regressed to ridicule myself for this crime. Where I counselled others to find their source of self-compassion, I was unwilling to let go of my self-hate. It breathed with me and was buried bone deep.

Angel had asked the most pertinent questions: what would I be without this pain? If it was not there, what would exist in its place? My mind turned to all the heartache that my pain had caused. Even though ambiguous, the abuse and what I perceived as the abandonment that came afterwards created aggravations that led to further assaults. My sense of faultiness flowed outwards and forged a path of fury. What if this seed of suffering had never been planted? What if this pain had never been propagated? What if I had been spared the sting of its poison and the stab of its thorns?

Without it, maybe my life would be regaled with many riches. It would be a life full of family and friends, and my girls would have a wider world of women to draw wisdom from. I would no longer be an outcast but a contributor to the clan. My mind would be freed from the effort of forgetting the immense immoralities that came from clambering through the chaos alone. I would be cleaner somehow. I could picture my insides looking like the cover of an interior design magazine; simple, stylish, serene, spotless, flawless. My hands would be bare, clear of the blood that I believed was baked on. My heart would be light, not laden with the foolish things I did to forget it. I could go about life knowing I was a good person. I could acknowledge my past and not have to avoid anyone.

It was funny how these thoughts overlapped with the first fortune cookie and its warning that principles are diluted with privilege. What if I had been parented by perfect people, constantly sheltered and supported and had slipped off the conveyer belt into adulthood, mentally stable. I am obsessed with the Law of opposites and the idea that there are two sides to every coin. So, with these gifts of goodness, what would have had to be given up? Of course, this exercise could only ever be hypothetical, but I could surmise that I would never have had to find my own solace. I never would have been forced to find the freedom I needed to interpret my own identity. Maybe always being able to rely on others would have made me lazy, less independent and less empathetic. For I could see that pain also came with the privilege of understanding our own darkness and therefore, that of others. I knew now that there was no simple black and white and that there could be a gentle existence within the grey. I was no longer lit in one dimension but understood the depth of my shadows. It was only by feeling the greatness of suffering that I could also sense how it was matched by my Spirit. Perhaps, without the pain, I would never have been open to Love or Angel or be lying here seeking answers that could help me become a better person. After all, was there really a difference between being a good person and becoming one? And can you consciously choose good if you have never known bad?

Mum and dad also had difficult upbringings, but I never saw them allow any self-pity. As a child, dad sometimes never knew where the next meal would come from and this had altered his approach to food. He too had adapted to ensure his survival. I did not recognise this in my childhood, cringing and ashamed every time he had to loosen his belt because he had eaten too much. But he never took any food for granted. Could it be what I thought gluttony was actually a form of gratefulness? Without being haunted by hunger, he would never have become so handy in the kitchen. Without shortage, he would never have grown so resourceful. I had seen how this lesson had been lost on me. Without scarcity, I had become wasteful. It was ironic how dad's efforts to provide us with plenty had, in a generation, eroded his ideals.

As one of the eldest children in a house of twelve, mum's income supplemented the sparse salaries of her parents. She cycled everywhere until she could save for a car and brought birthday gifts for the younger siblings that her parents could not afford. She transformed her efforts into special times, ensuring birthdays were marked with brightened hearts and beaming faces. Even in the last few months of her life, she still sent cards and lottery tickets to those blessed to be in her birthday book. It sat upon the corner shelf; its red leather cover bent but robust, old but obvious. Without being compelled to find a way to contribute, she would not have known the rewards that come with generosity, and many lives would have been poorer as a result.

Both worked hard to survive and to provide the life and luxury they wanted for their children. It led to exhausting days, late nights and absences that I sometimes misconstrued as acts of cruelty. But without being born into this, I would never have known the benefits of hard work. I would be devoid of the discipline that now allows me to create financial freedom for my family. While I share the frustrating trait of turning everything into work, without this rigour, our family would struggle to pay for food, let alone school fees. One night, when my father was in one of his annual rampages, I was stupid enough to ask him what was more important, his family or his work. Without hesitation he replied it was the latter because it put food on our table. I had judged him harshly for this answer, thinking him callous and uncaring. Now I understand how tenuous the ties are between work and family. At the time, I thought the question was righteous, but now I know it was ultimately unfair.

Without Secret, there would not be Shame. And without Shame, there would not be Pain. But without Pain, there would be no compulsion towards Providence.

The second question Angel asked instigated my imagination. With all of these wounds, who could I be? Instead of wasting my energy on wallowing in the mud, who could I build from the bricks?

The psychic had seen distress in my mother's eyes, yet at her funeral, the church had overflowed. Somehow, she had found a way to channel her afflictions and transform them into acts of kindness and connection. I always used to be embarrassed when she would talk to people in the supermarket or stop to compliment people on the street. Now, I am honoured to do it on her behalf. This thought came with a great swell of sadness. I wish I had seen the beauty in her behaviour when she was alive so I could have expressed my admiration. I can only hope she would appreciate the ignorance that came with my immaturity. I had no idea where she was now, but I whispered to her anyway, "Mum, you are amazing."

I was expecting a similar sizable crowd for dad's service tomorrow. However, in the last twenty years, many of his friends have already moved on or are far less mobile. No doubt, though, there would be many there ready to testify to the good man that he was. He found a way to work through his heaps of hurt, and now there would be hundreds coming to honour him.

It was fair to say that dad had inherited forceful opinions about the folly of feelings. He was taught that artistic pursuits were lazy, emotions were the enemy, and that work was the only way to salvation; you only achieved legacy through hard labour. The result was a body and heart that suffered from a complete lack of self-compassion and a constrained palette of creative colours. Yet he channelled this conflict into care for others and blended within the boundaries to create beauty. He sacrificed his time, energy, money and materials so that others could find comfort. He exhausted himself for my education and worked tirelessly to support my travels, a sacrifice whose significance I can only now begin to sense. Yet he never wanted to be seen as a martyr. Instead, he was satisfied with the thought that he had expanded my world and aided my adventures, and lived vicariously through my voyages. Through his sense of wonder and excitement at my explorations, I had come to see that we were much more similar than I could ever have understood as a child.

The message written on the fortune cookie fell into place. Some days, I still saw the black, grimy fingerprints of my father, left from when he would force down my fullness. But besides these, there are marks that made magic, opened a world of wonder, and built internal strength, independence, and imagination. It was now up to me to choose which fingerprints to let fade, and which ones to reinforce.

I'M SORRY JUNO

Chapter 7

The morning was morose, full of sombre questions and monosyllabic answers. I made porridge in honour of Poppy, with the girls only able to eat a bit of brown sugar. Still, it was a fitting tribute to the many mornings when Poppy's serving of the sweet, creamy warmth was met with smiles. Outfits were ironed, makeup exchanged, and hair plaited. I had forgotten to buy black ribbon which I regretted, but saw the wisdom in my purchase of waterproof mascara. Unlike when I was at their age, my girls had very little black clothing. As a teenager, I would have been classed as an Emo, with a wardrobe drenched in darkness. These girls, though, were only ever encased in pastels and vanilla hues. Their dad had to take them shopping for fitting funeral outfits, a fashion expedition that held no fun. I always knew they had a special style and would find something that suited them and the occasion. They stood here now, beautiful in black.

On the way to the church, we stopped at the printers. I held it together as we looked through the brochure over the counter, and I complimented the designer's work. But opening the boot sent forth a barrage of brutality. Seeing dad's photo on the page, along with the date of his death, suddenly made it all seem real. And I had realised how thin the veneer of my acceptance was. The tears flowed into a flood, and my sadness was contagious. Soon, all three of us had stopped trying to hold them back and allowed our bodies to succumb to their own sense of sanity. When the storm subsided, we held each other through the wreckage and guided each other in cleaning our eyes. I may not have remembered ribbons, but I had compensated with a handbag full of tissues and wet wipes.

Even with our unplanned, pre-funeral purge, we were still early to the church but too late to see the entrance of dad's coffin. It sat so regally, adorned by wreaths and a photo of the man who meant so much. We divided the brochures along the seats and left the rest for the ushers to give to those who would be standing. Then we took our place in the front pew, where forty years ago, I knelt and prayed to be a nun. While my parents and siblings sat, religiously, in the second back row and right against the wall, I would go to the front and beside the aisle to be closer to the action. It seemed so simple now, but back then, I honestly believed I would gain some favours from being closer to the cross. This routine only lasted a few months. When my public piety did not deliver superior maths results, my dedication was ditched. I returned to the rear to resume my seat, situated only slightly in front of the children's tantrum room.

Today, though, my sister and I were both here at the front, but at extreme ends. We were soon shielded from each other by dad's sisters; getting the support we needed but which we were unwilling to give to each other. My brother entered and seated himself at the aisle, ready to do his duty as pallbearer. We waited as the singers rehearsed, the people piled in, speakers checked the state of the microphones, and booklets became fans. Glancing behind, I saw my cousin seated behind his mother with his hand on her shoulder. I could not, or would not, look at him, not out of anger, but of apathy. This time was too important to waste on a worry that would wait. We stood to sing the opening hymn, the musical version of the Serenity Prayer. I had chosen it to act as an invitation, asking Serenity, Courage and Wisdom to come forth and stand beside us all.

God grant me the serenity
to accept the things I cannot change;
courage to change the things I can;
and wisdom to know the difference.

Singing these lines made me reflect on the wisdom that Angel had suggested already lived within. I knew he was here, too, honouring his word. At that moment, I realised what was truly important. I cuddled my girls close, held their hands, and tried to pass on the Love I had experienced from their grandparents and the angel that had gone with them.

The ceremony was simple and short, just as dad would have wanted it; he was not one for pomp and pageantry, happy with a humble display. Seeing all the attendees, the priest no longer needed to rely on my account of the man we were there to farewell. The generous turnout was a testament to this truth. Dad's sisters did a reading each, showing their strength through shaky voices. The eulogy was delivered by an uncle, often chosen for such occasions due to his superior oratory. Through it all, we sat in silence, one broken only by syncopated sniffles.

At the finale of the formalities, my brother met with his mates at the coffin, shook hands with every comrade and then each took turns grabbing a handle. I did not know any of the guys in the guard, but I was warmed by what they wore. They had gone to great lengths to look professional, and I know it would have made dad proud. I remember seeing dad balk when I presented my daughter for her christening on a hot summer's day in bare feet. He could rest safely now, knowing he was surrounded by those dressed in respect.

The front-row families followed the sleepy procession. I could not help but think how unlike this walk was to my wedding. The two occasions shared the same site, but their emotions were at the opposite extremes. My wedding was awash with white, shiny, sparkling decor, with every detail meticulously planned over months. Walking up the aisle, I met the eyes of all the guests, smiling with the expectation and excitement of my new status. I wanted everyone to see me, celebrate me, and acknowledge my normality.

Today, I could hardly see past my tears and was bedecked in black. I no longer wore the ring of engagement and walked wearily from a program that had been pieced together in days. I wished I did not have to be seen and that I could escape this show. Just then, I remembered what the director had said.

"Funerals are not for the dead, they are for the living."

There were many more lives here than my own that needed a place to process their grief, and so I admonished myself for my self-absorption.

My wedding and this funeral, though, did meet in the middle around a shared sense of uncertainty. When I was getting married, I had no idea what the future would be like, bound to another. This time, I could not comprehend what my life would be like when bonds that began at birth were broken.

As we shuffled forward, I heard the final song I had selected. This was not chosen for the dead man, but as a desperate instruction for his daughter.

Lord, make me an instrument of your peace.
Where there is hatred, let me sow love;
where there is injury, pardon;
where there is doubt, faith;
where there is despair, hope;
where there is darkness, light;
and where there is sadness, joy.
O Divine Master, grant that I may not so much seek
to be consoled as to console;
to be understood as to understand;
to be loved as to love.
For it is in giving that we receive;
it is in pardoning that we are pardoned;
and it is in dying that we are born to eternal life.

The travel between the church and the cemetery was shrouded in silence. I could not tell if it came from a place of settlement or suppression, relief or reinforcement, capitulation or trepidation, or all the above.

We stood beside the grave and were given peonies in a celebration of colour. These fantastic flowers honoured all the seed packets dad kept on the kitchen bench and which he had grown in his garden. On previous visits, over tea, dad and I had chatted about the curious mix of plant names, ranging from the obvious colour titles, such as Coral Charm, to those named in tributes to great entertainers, for example, the Shirley Temple. I wondered what criteria the company used to choose people to name their flowers after. What filters did they use to find those who were fitting representatives? Then I contemplated, when asked, what colour I would want to be associated with. I found my conceit comical and delighted then in my self-deprecation. Why on earth would anyone associate me with something so precious?

The stems we held beside dad's grave were simply exquisite, enchanting in their complexity. Each petal fitted perfectly in the pattern. I remembered once trying to repair a rose by removing a single discoloured petal on the periphery. With this one slight change I had spoiled its perfection, and no matter how many I tried to remove to correct my error, it never did look right.

There was little ritual before the coffin began to be lowered. We followed the priest's sprinkling of the holy water with our offering of the perfect peonies. I knew which contribution I considered more important. At that moment, though, Memory marauded through again, echoing the cries from my nephew at my mother's funeral. An Aunty had told the toddler to toss the rose to his Nana. His eyes went wild, and he screamed, "Is Nan down there?". From there, he was inconsolable, acting out in ways I wish I could have. The cacophony broadcast the extent of internal chaos, and I wondered if this same confusion was churning within my daughters.

At the wake, we sat awkwardly, which I reflected was appropriate given we were not adept at attending such events or taking part in public gatherings. A steady stream of well-wishers came to offer their condolences and comfort, but with each one that passed, I began to feel further out of my depth. I did not know most and could only introduce a few by name. I had to curb my self-criticism but was saved by my brother coming to stand beside us and the girls' cousins sitting with us, creating a sense of collegiality. I knew everyone's words were said with respect, but soon, the reprisal of, "sorry for your loss" became stale. The repeated reminder of our deprivation did little to ease the discomfort. I wondered what one could say to a person that would still show empathy but, instead of stating what had been lost, shift the focus to what had been gained. "You were lucky to have him in your life for as long as you did," may have been an option. But who was I kidding, no words would ever reduce the agony.

And then I saw the offender off in the distance. He was helping his mother heap up some plates with sandwiches and slices. Secret was standing in his shadow. It was so hard not to consider his grief a ruse and a form of goading. But I would not break dad's honour and confront this culprit, so I spent the rest of the time there doing what was already well-rehearsed, avoiding and pretending he did not exist. In reality, I continued to see him caring for his mother. Making her coffee, sharing tissues and then supporting her to be seated safely in the car. I could turn my back on these things, confine them to the corners of my eyes, but I could not unsee them.

I found people tiring at the best of times, but playing host all afternoon was a gruelling mission. People were so generous, sharing stirring stories of dad, some of which we had never heard. It made me think that I should have begun his biography when I had the chance. Yes, Shame was also there, not to pay tribute but to stir those perturbed by broken promises. Others professed praise and pride for us, and we stumbled over some small talk to smooth over the distance. At some point, though, I disengaged, unsure whether my daughters had beaten me to it. I gave up working hard to honour each conversation and allowed myself to slip into the haze.

I had, until my conversation with Angel, shared the view of my psych that dissociation was a disorder. That my ability to sever from myself was a further sign of instability. Now, I found it a valuable skill to fight off overwhelm. What was worse? Option one, my mind wandering off to another world. Or option two, a crazed conversation followed by public rants and riots? Today, I had seen how many things I had previously judged harshly as sensitivities offer sagacity. What I once saw as cowardice now came forth as a clever creator of comfort. Where before I would chastise myself for these flaws, I began thanking them for their attempts at assistance.

I began to understand what Angel meant when he said he could not override my own sense of self-protection. I was starting to see how dangerous and destructive this may be.

Back at the cottage, no one felt like leftover soggy sandwiches, and no one was tempted by the thought of them transformed into toasties. We joined in the ritual of makeup removal and then took turns showering. We sought sympathy in our pyjamas, with me pondering out loud about how clothes could provide so much comfort. My daughters did not even try to answer, well-versed in my propensity for rhetoric, and too weary to share in my wondering.

We had some cake and hot chocolate and then curled up together in Poppy's bed. Re-enacting nights from years ago seemed like a trivial but fitting tribute. Being so close to each other, while cramped, also cultivated calm. Our arms woven together kept us from worry. Beside my girls, listening to them breathing, I had never been anywhere more beautiful.

I'M SORRY JUNO

Chapter 8

Snug and exhausted, we all slept soundly, rousing well after sunrise and then only slowly. The girls started their day staring at social media. I shuffled into the kitchen to make tea. Neither child was hungry yet, so I had a few minutes to sip, set my intention and steel myself for the day. Every night before bed, my mother would ready the teapot for the next day, a habit I had originally seen as unnecessary and to be honest, a little OCD. However, I have come to also cherish this practice, realising it provides two clear rewards. The first is that it closes the day and provides a perfect transition to bedtime. As the pot is positioned next to the kettle, and the cup is covered I can celebrate overcoming the day's challenges. Then in the morning, these items provide an important reminder of my first mission; make the tea, and everything else will move into place. Just like the Disney characters I watched as a child, the teapot greets me with motherly support saying, "You've got this". The cup joins in with, "Let's go, girlfriend!" These were not just items on the shelf but a shrine to the self. I know it is much more than tea; it is a token of faith.

The minutes to mid-morning were filled with pacing, picking, plonking and packing. The girls would return home this evening to be greeted by a generous grandmother I knew would attend to their needs. In the early days of the divorce, my mother-in-law kept her distance. However, when she realised I still cared for her child and that I had succeeded in casting out my addiction, we reinstated our mutual respect. She loved the girls greater than if they were the daughters she never had. Whenever they returned home from a visit at grandma's, the girls would pine for her porridge and glorify her gravy. While her ability to aid them academically had long passed, she taught them lessons for a lifetime, including what it feels like to be truly loved. Despite their desire to stay the remaining two days and return with me, their commitments were more important than my company. They had friends and teachers who understood their anguish, and they had each other.

My sister shuffled through the back door, followed by her daughter. I had seen them approaching along the path well-worn by my footsteps. The strip of Earth between my childhood home and the cottage took only a few minutes to traverse. Yet within it was embedded the whole range of human emotions. This was a transitional track, where we each prepared for what was to come or tried to placate ourselves from what had just passed. I don't remember ever simply strolling along this street enjoying casual, comfortable chats. It was usually spent speeding along in silence. And this is how I had seen my sister on every previous visit. She seemed always to have a pressing purpose, her stride swift and her face firm. Today, though, her usual committed pace was a challenge. It was as if she was fighting against some invisible force or being withheld by a headwind. My sister's fury was also muted. She looked so old and so tired. I knew the exhaustion of Anger, but when layered with Grief, there was not much room left for vitality.

There were no hugs, just hollow hellos.

"How are you?", was met with, "I'm okay."

These responses were well-rehearsed. I had learned that overt expressions of emotions were not encouraged and replies that referenced them were never well-regarded. No one was ever "great," only "good". No one was ever brilliant, just "not bad". None of us was ever fantastic, only "fair to middling". Exuberance was considered excessive and boasting a dreadful display of indulgence. Years on, I had also come to know that beliefs build your reality and words colour your world. Through our rejoinders, we created a range of restrictions and repressed both the bright and dark. I understand that such moderation was then considered a sign of maturity, but now I cannot help but think this culture was simply cruel.

After some friendlier formalities, the daughter joined her cousins on the couch to begin the search for common ground. There was nothing I could provide for my sister, which was normal. She had already had tea, didn't eat cake, didn't feel like fruit and didn't want to sit down. I wondered if it was only my offerings she found repugnant or whether she rejected treats presented by other relatives. When we were at home, I saw how often my girls would share clothes, jewellery and makeup. This was in stark contrast to my childhood. My sister built a compound around her possessions and there would be clashes if I crossed the boundary. Sure, my daughters sometimes denied requests or met my demands for sharing with spite. But as well as conflict, their chattels were also a source of connection.

Instead of staying to talk, she went to begin auditing the garage, notepad and pen ready for the stocktake of what would be destroyed, sold, or donated. The task provided some relief, and the activity was a pleasant escape from my annoying presence.

The creation of my own action list was cut short with the arrival of my brother and cuddles, coffees and concise chats around the kitchen bench. The girls' sombre eyes were raised momentarily from their screens to spy on their uncle, and then their bodies were torn from the seats to share a hug. He spurred an interest, which, while sporadic, was still an improvement over inertia. My sister also seemed to sense the need to engage the girls and encourage their contribution. She brought them a pile of photo albums and, as they flicked through the pages, they began to forge pathways with foreign faces and make fun of their fashions. The images brought them close to their ancestry, the people and places that had shaped their spirits. My sister's gifts created curiosity and a range of questions, pulling her to participate. While tense, there was still a sense of togetherness that felt like a triumph.

My sister came to stand and the bench and declared that we needed to discuss what to do with the cottage. As I suspected, my siblings supported its sale. Neither needed more to worry about, and the financial aid would be appreciated. I shared these sentiments and asked how I could be of service in the process. It was not lost on me, though, that without this place, the girls and I would no longer have a reason to visit or a residence to return to. The last link to their lineage would be lost, and we would have to find alternative holiday aims and accommodation. I only wished that the secret this house held could also be sold with all strings severed with a simple signature. I knew, though, that Secret and Shame held no allegiance to an abode and were both invisible and inside of me. They could not be consigned to others via contract, but, I wondered, could they be settled?

With a break in the conversation, my brother took the chance to ask if the girls would like a ride on his motorbike. He had brought an extra helmet and could take them for a hoon in the paddock behind the house. I could see the initial resistance and concern on my children's faces. Could they have fun when they have just attended their grandfather's funeral? Was it respectful to experience pleasure when you are still mourning your grandparent's passing? Could the two co-exist, or would it create too much internal conflict? I simplified their struggle by giving my permission and confirming that now was the perfect time before it got too hot. My motherly instinct was mortified, and I began imagining the many mortal wounds they may sustain. But logic was louder, reminding me that I cannot hold them back from the fullness of life. Instead of rejection, I had learnt the art of risk management, and in this activity, I trusted both parties.

How lucky these girls were to have someone to provide answers, even if they only became opinions they chose to oppose. I no longer had my mother to endorse a course of action or provide the trusted consent I could not give myself. So many times, I had wished she was there to ask for advice. Her loss had created a sense of loneliness and had me often feeling sorry for myself. I had crafted a constant narrative of abandonment. It was a story formed by years of self-reinforcement and one-sided observations. Now, here I was, even more than motherless; I was an orphan. And yet Angel had suggested that alternate and less acrid tales also existed and that these were readily available. Instead of a single, determined ending, I was the main character in a choose-your-own-adventure.

This thought sent me forward from the solitary space to stand beside my sister, listing and sorting possessions into piles. I wondered if she, too, was tired of the tension. Perhaps it was time to try another way.

"Thanks for everything you did for Dad."

How contrasting this was to a conversation held a decade ago, which, if I were honest, was more of a drunken rant. Between talk and texts, I had berated her for being a bitch and treating our father terribly. I had accused her of taking advantage of his generosity, stopping short of suggesting elder abuse. Still, it hung in the air, ready to attack anytime. This was the last lengthy exchange and one which Memory had recorded clearly in my mind. At the time I remember feeling so righteous, my judgement so justified. But for many years since, I have used this scene as a source of self-flagellation, never considering seeking Forgiveness.

A purposeful pause.

An intentional inhalation.

Both caution and care for what may come next.

"I am so sorry for everything I did when I was sick. I know it was all disgusting and I am really sorry."

I felt no need to spell out individual instances of our horrible interactions. Presenting the plethora of examples would only extend the pain and be counterproductive to any sense of peace. It would be like rubbing sharp salt crystals into wounds that were still raw and weeping. From a more practical perspective, there were also probably far too many of my evil events to list, and I was aware there could be more I was unable or unwilling to remember. If I didn't know why I woke up pantless on my lawn at midnight, then it was likely the phone call listed on the log was just as pathetic.

For the smallest second, our eyes met. This span of time in which we shared sight was miniscule, but it felt momentous. For decades, we had looked in the general direction of the other, but past their person, never stopping to actually see our sister.

She gave a small nod of acknowledgement and then moved away to assess another area. I was not stupid enough to think my single brick could bridge the sinkhole that was our sisterhood. But perhaps it could play some part in revising our roles so that we could both play the part of adults. Casting me as the child and her as the parent had only led to contempt.

Minutes went by while we each processed the experience.

Then she spoke.

"Are you okay now?"

Those four words were covered with a translucent cloak, clear enough to let through some light.

"Yes, I'm solid."

I impressed myself with my choice of words. It was expressive but not excessive, revealing but not dramatic, meaningful but not emotional. It told of being able to be trusted, of being in a place where a reconstruction could be possible and visits would be assured of safety.

"Let's get coffee".

These simple words suggested that my sister understood and they also held a trace of commendation.

We shared a dislike of instant coffee and discussed the places in town that were good options for future outings. It was a staid conversation, comfortable in its solemnity. However, within I could feel a force growing. A question was poking, prodding and being pushed upwards. I no longer had the power to suppress my curiosity and yearning to know. Angel had told me that other perspectives were already present, and I had one now sitting opposite me. It was an opportunity I could no longer afford to overlook and a prize I would no longer pass over.

This moment felt like the daring deeds I had done in the past, and that demanded action without delay. An iota more thought and the momentum would be lost, like jumping off a high platform into a murky dam. Or sliding into the rapids to be washed down a waterfall. I had not yet braved bungee or skydiving but imagined it would require the same rejection of rumination. One could rightly argue that much mischief was made through the detangling of thought and action, but it also enabled the greatest experiments. If one stopped wasting time surmising what failure would look like, they would be free to find out. Believing and Knowing were two different beasts.

Shame sat beside me, whispering its warning to "shut up." But my sister had seen much worse than this.

"Could I ask a question? It is about something that has been eating away at me since I was a child. Do you remember anything happening between me and Brett over here when I was in kindy? I think something sexual went on and I thought you might have stopped it. I have just been trying to piece it together."

The vagueness, once a vicissitude, now created a valuable space for my sister's story. My confusion seemed to cast her with calm, and my lack of surety was met with strength. She sedately shocked me by saying that, on several occasions, our cousin had commanded her to touch his private parts. He had pulled them out, presented them to her, and made her play with them. I did not delve into what compelled her to comply, for I knew this invisible force intimately.

Then, she relayed another revelation. She knew he did something to our other cousin Jennifer, but was sparse on specifics, and I was averse to asking further.

My sister, though, did not remember anything about me being embroiled in such behaviour.

I asked her if she recalled any problems with me pooing my pants or if she knew of any surgery I went through to stop this shame. Somewhere in my mind, Memory had planted this as a possibility; that my anus had been extended to allow easier passage of the excrement. I found no evidence of this, and it seemed like an extreme and horrific response to age-regressive behaviours. And yet, it was stuck in my psyche and a constant reminder of just how warped my Memory was. In months past, I went down many research rabbit holes seeking confirmation that my faecal soiling could have been evidence of sexual abuse. The only academic confirmation I could find was that such behaviours were a sign, but more commonly just a symptom of generalised stressors. There was no causation between the two curses. Yet I surely thought something as serious as a hospital visit could be a significant memory for my sister, so if it did happen, she should know.

But all she could attest to was that she, too, had often pooed her pants.

So, I was not singularly stupid. The siblings had both suffered stressors.

There was no more to be said. In a few long minutes, we learned so much about our shared worries. A crumb of conflict had been replaced with collegiality, and we had found some common enemies. My absolute antagonist had transformed into a partial ally. And all I had to do was ask.

Although the rest of the sorting session was spent in silence, I had relief roaring in my heart. I felt Secret shrinking and Shame fretting about its tenancy. My sister's answers, while short and still misty, proved there was a pattern that supported my version of events. It had abated my need for acknowledgement and advised that I was not alone. Knowing others also got caught and corrupted lessened the belief that it was just me that was broken. Yes, I was sad for their suffering, and I knew this would become more intense if I investigated further. But right then, I was enjoying the selfish satisfaction of knowing that Secret had been shared and congratulating myself for my courage. I had replaced repression with reaching out and suppression with speaking out. It was only a little leap, but I felt like it had created the potential for flight. And the connection, while scant and based on the sinister, was a gentle and genuine gift to my father's ghost.

I heard my daughters bounding through the back door, babbling to their uncle, unified by adventure. In my presence, they seemed to downsize their delight, but I could still see they were enthralled and energised. I was so glad they got to experience the giddiness of going at great speed and the pleasure of being the passenger of a professional. I knew of the crazy combination of excitement and ease that came with being on the back of a motorbike. A few years ago, my now ex-boyfriend would pick me up each Sunday morning, and we would head out for hours through the mountains and grab coffee at the markets.

Before embarking, though, he would inspect my clothing, securing all the straps and ensuring I was tucked in tight. The attention was almost parental and definitely perfectionist, but I found his care precious as if he believed I was.

I would cuddle into him as we curved and bumped helmets when he unexpectedly braked. The breeze against my body was beautiful and beckoned me to open to all around me. There was no separation between the self and the scene, which stirred all my senses. Every time I see a couple cruising, I realise how much I miss this companionship and the convenient relief that came when someone else did the driving.

One day, while coming down from this ecstasy, I considered the ease with which I entrusted my physical form to the missions and mischiefs of the men in my life but the excruciating lengths I would use to prevent them from entering my internal world. Perhaps this was a lesson learned when little, that my body was dispensable and a dependable distraction. It allowed me to profess participation while still holding the power to protect my spirit. This tangent of thought illuminated yet another insight. I prided myself on how well I protected my true self from other people, but punished them when they were not proficient enough to penetrate my armour. Vulnerability was something I had come to associate with violation and violence, but I was now being asked to accept that it could be a virtue.

As I made stacks of shirts, I listed the strengths of keeping these safeguards, finding several justifications for staying the same. Then, while folding the pants, I considered the option of openness, of relieving the defenders of their duty and having confidence in my own care. The experience with my sister showed that if I let someone in, I would still exist and that being with someone would not always create wounds. The latter was a possibility when I found someone I could trust. Then I remembered the answer that I could not articulate with Angel but was acknowledged by my awkward silence. There is no trust for others until you can trust yourself.

For a considerable time, I wondered if there was any other way. I called on my cleverness to find a way in which I could give to others generously without opening any gates, one that lent itself to an outpouring of love without letting any in. There must be a way to outsmart the Law of Opposites! What about a closed city with one-way roads. Or an open system with inbuilt intelligent obstructions. I could love freely, but when alarms were sounded, launch a lockdown. But trying to come up with the criteria for knowing when the closure was constructive and not just convenient became problematic. Then, coming up with indicators for reopening was confusing. My daughter was kind enough to cease the chaos that came with this thinking, saying it was almost time to go.

We had agreed to join my aunties and their families for a late lunch before my daughters' flight. My sister had declined, doubting her ability to stand all the fuss. When I asked my brother, he replied, "I would rather shoot myself." It was an awful analogy but an accurate portrayal of what we were all thinking. It sounded like a wonderful idea for my children to spend time with family in a friendlier setting and a wonderful chance for me to think about one less meal. But for a moment, I entertained the idea of cancelling. I could cite an oncoming cold. My aunties old age would make this seem less of a rejection and more an act of regard. Still, this was a small sacrifice to make for my father's siblings. While dad would likely have opted out, he would be pleased to know that our tribe was there, providing representation and support. So, the girls' bags were piled into the car; they cuddled their aunt, uncle and cousin and left the cottage for maybe the last time.

"Will we ever come back?", my daughter asked woefully when we were on our way.

"I really don't know what the future looks honey. But for now, just know that Poppy is much more than just this place."

I thought of the fortune cookie and fingerprints and imagined my father placing his thumb on my daughters' foreheads and making a shiny imprint showing how much they were cherished.

My Aunt's house smelt like a strange mix of meatballs and lavender. I surmised the former was for the feast, but the latter was for her desolation. Her husband had died only a year before, leaving her alone for the first time in well over fifty years. Now, she was also laden with the loss of her little brother. The scent was a puny support for the size of sadness she was shouldering, but it was better than nothing and showed some small semblance of self-compassion. The purple perfume was also a perfect match to the décor. My Aunt had a love for violets, and they were everywhere. China and crystal versions were in the display cabinets, cotton ones captured on cushions, and embroidered ones on the apron she wore. I thought if I decided to collect anything, it would be teapots. But I could never see myself being that single-minded, passionate or wealthy.

When we arrived, though, her only concern was introducing us to the extended family. There were great-grandchildren, second and third cousins, partners, and a few pets. The menagerie was a little overwhelming, and I felt my girls move close beside me. After the formalities, my Aunt called us forward into a small bedroom. There before us on the beds were lots of pretty boxes. Some were large, square and sparkly. Others were oval and embroidered or bedazzled with brightness. A few were wonderfully simple, woven in white, while some small ones were silver and there were a couple that were carved.

"I couldn't wait for you to come to choose your presents. Please, help yourself. The other girls have had their turn, so take whatever you want. I know you have to put in all in your luggage, but there is plenty there that won't break." She placed a kiss on each of the girls' heads and left to continue cooking.

She really was remarkable. Even Grief could not stop her giving. Selflessness seemed to run in the family. The girls didn't remember the last time they had sat on these beds. It was a Christmas when they were just toddlers, and there were bags full of dolls, games, little books and puzzles. The children had loaded up everything they loved and then Aunty sent us off with a stack of snacks; juice boxes, biscuits, chips and lollies. She was an endless source of extravagance. The girls were eager to explore and dived into the adventure, their discomfort consoled by the cache. If Aunty had stayed, their inspection would have been much timider, but alone, they were authentically avaricious. In the big boxes were bric-a-brac, trinkets and a mountain of makeup samples. The lesser containers held a carnival of costume jewellery and crystals. Aunty returned with a bag for them each, apologising for forgetting to bring them sooner, and hurried away, saying, "Happy hunting". Dad had told me that Aunty made an easter egg hunt in her front yard for the neighbourhood children every year and always had a pile of Halloween treats waiting at her door. Here was a lady who loved large, and I could almost see the light that trailed behind her.

This treasure hunt was so different from what I experienced as a child. With the passing of both of mum's parents, the elder's possessions were gathered, and the most valuable was shared among the siblings. The bits left over were offered to the grandchildren. All of the cousins gathered together and were tasked with choosing a memento of people we never really knew. I was drawn to the oddities, walking away with an ashtray shaped like a skull and a bright pink bobbly bottle opener. I never used either for their intended purposes; they were just displayed on my dressing table. Thinking about them now, I wonder if they represented my predilection for the peculiar or whether they were predictions of my future dependencies.

I was relieved when the girls' choices were finalised without conflict. History had taught me there was the possibility of overlap in what they wanted, which would breed contempt at best and conflict at worst. It would usually conclude with my eldest conceding and my youngest silently strutting. These usually led to conversations encouraging my eldest to user her voice to get what she wanted. But she is far more clever than that. She has chosen a calmer way, forging paths of individuality that no one else can follow. As younger children, this copycat behaviour from my youngest was prolific, and I began to understand why my sister may have loathed me so much. No matter how much I advocated to my eldest that mimicry was the highest form of acclaim, the constant flattery only led to frustration. I cannot remember ever looking up to my sister. But where there is hatred, there is also admiration, even only as a possibility.

Even after all the treasure was brandished and bagged, we opted to stay in the room.

"Can we not stay long, please Mama."

These were pleas that were often present at any sort of social gathering or public outing. Certainly, a lack of practice would make mingling cumbersome and not a comfortable choice. Each had perfected protocols and pleasantries but held no desire to engage, entertain or enquire about others. I wondered whether this was another sign of the "age of entitlement" that an elder had presented as a reason for their self-orientation or whether this restraint was a mark of reverence for their closest role model. I was happy in my isolation, hated small talk, and felt nervous around noise and chaotic in crowds. Maybe instead of finding their resistance irksome, I should take it as a form of imitation and idolatry. If I found their preferences problematic, what judgements was I also making about the person who inspired them?

Our chit-chat was interrupted by my other Aunt, who came, sat, and asked how we were doing. She was almost the polar opposite of the host, speaking softly, seriously and dressed precisely. She asked how the girls were doing in school and whether they played sports. She congratulated their choices of hockey and touch football, believing they were both courageous. She asked how my writing was going. I desperately wanted to tell her my ideas for a novel about our famous ancestors. But before I could begin, I decided it best not to induce interest in something that may never transpire. I mentioned that I was experimenting with fiction after a string of books about real events. She grabbed my hands and said, "Just keep going. It is so wonderful to have an author in the family." I smiled but wondered if this praise would be as plentiful if she knew I was merely self-published?

This lamentation was interrupted by the lunch bell, and Aunty bundled us out to the backyard. The lavishness of my larger Aunt was laid out across two tables, with smaller ones spotted across the lawn, surrounded by plastic chairs. We were encouraged to "dig in", and only then remembered how much I despised eating in public. I would have refrained if it had not been taken as an insult, but my Aunt prided herself on full plates. I shot the girls a look of sympathy, hoping they saw it progress to pleading. Luckily, no prompting or pressure was needed. The spread was both simple and special. The salads were stylish and easily swamped a plate. The girls took their fill of finger food, fascinated by the spectrum of sauces, and then we found the table furthest away and sat. While I was still feeling a little nervous, it was now matched by relief.

Until I saw THE cousin, Brett. He came up beside Jennifer at the serving tables and said something short. She pretended he did not exist, didn't even look at him. She kept her head down and rushed away, her plate only holding one small pile of potato salad. I knew then what my sister had heard was honest. Usual sins would be met with malice or spite, but sexual abuse always spawned suppressed shame. Perhaps he was on the prowl, or the seat next to me was the last available place. Either way, he came and sat so close I could smell his cologne. His mere presence was another act of contempt. I defaulted to freeze mode, bending down to pretend to buckle my shoe while trying to recall how to breathe. I would not make a scene here in front of my children, nor could I with limbs that had become icy cold, contrasting the searing shame seeping through my cheeks. I sat up and saw the slight shock on my girl's face. I was no longer the woman they walked over to the table with.

"Are you alright, Mama?", the eldest asked.

"Yes honey, a bit of salad just went down the wrong way."

I took a sip of water to solidify the excuse, but my girls were not that stupid. They stared at the man in our midst until I mentioned they should finish their lunches because we would need to leave soon.

Brett was painfully pleasant. He introduced himself to the girls and told them that he was the man who had bought all their Poppy's cows.

My youngest simply responded, "Well you better bloody take care of them."

At that moment, I realised I had other protectors in my presence, and my limbs lost a little of their chill.

My heart sang, "You go girl!" but not loud enough for anyone to hear. Instead, I stood, slung my bag over my shoulder, grabbed our almost empty plates and said, "Excuse us, we need to get the girls to their flight."

We were far too early for the airport, but this tale had some semblance of truth. At least one girl needed to get away immediately. A further delay in departure may produce the dangerous actions my doctor had predicted.

On the way out we went and hugged the aunties and provided our thanks. They expressed their joy that we had joined them, and their delight defrosted me a little further. I said a separate goodbye to Jennifer, unsure if my sister had spoken to her but needing to show my support. With my hand on her back, I looked across to Brett, hoping he would see this subtle display of solidarity. But he was gone, either to gloat alone or to avoid appearing abandoned. It was a stark reminder that this was no show, and no-one got to play the superhero.

With our early exit we had missed dessert, and with Time producing a spacious and peaceful presence, we headed to the ice cream parlour and the park. We found a seat not covered in duck crap and licked and crunched our way through the waffle cones; vanilla for the youngest, rainbow for the eldest, and raspberry for me.

Our silent savouring, and private thoughts were interrupted by my eldest, who could no longer censor her concern or stifle her curiosity.

"Mum, you looked really upset."

While she had made a statement, it sat more like a question. Stating the obvious was her method for enticing an explanation. It was clever and effective, and I accepted her invitation.

"I really don't like Brett. I think he may have taken advantage of Poppy and not paid enough for the cows."

Dad had never suggested anything of the sort. Certainly, there was no proof, but given past patterns, it was plausible.

"It was just a bit hard to be near him. Sorry we took off so early."

My apologies were met with affirmations. She said she was glad to go. While it was nice to know they had a big family, she preferred to spend more time with me.

This made me think about family and how, despite it being represented clearly in the dictionary, it was, in reality, an individual interpretation. I had tried to fabricate the idealised form but failed; I could not successfully sustain the advertised standard. So, I designed my own definition but also became determined to allow its evolution.

With our relatively sedate sugar highs, we drove to the airport. The eldest played music, which was not usually remarkable, but given the situation, this time was meaningful. There was a definite difference, though. Usually, the volume would border on violence, which I would either ignore or engage with as a way to re-energise. Some days, I would dance in my seat, onlookers enjoying a show while my girls slumped embarrassed in their seats. On other days, so much was happening in my head that it did not sound like music but more mayhem. My attempt to turn down the volume was a clear message that mum was not in the mood for a party but was preoccupied with self-protection. During this trip, instead of manifesting a mosh-pit, the soundtrack meandered through the atmosphere, not demanding attention but happy to be a modest companion.

By the time we reached the airport and went through check-in, we did not have long to wait. This was good given there were sparse retail diversions and sitting around would have just felt awkward. Neither of the girls felt like reading, and their sweet teeth were already sedated. So, to soak up Time, the girls took turns showing me the latest fashion trends on social media. In between, I watched the baggage handlers loading the planes and wondered what worries were in each of those suitcases. For even on the most exciting of adventures, the most sought-after trips, you still had to take the self.

With the call for first-class passengers, the tears commenced, and I handed over packets of tissues. With the general call, we tied ourselves into tight hugs, only separating when the line was sparse. I missed them the moment they went through the door. There is an energy that springs from them that enlivens me. Their presence compels me to enact my purpose. I have spent much time finding this source within myself, but as yet have not uncovered anything as magnificent as their magic.

Yet I was glad the girls had gone; I did not want them to witness what would come next.

As their plane took flight, I knew all that was left was fight.

The winds picked up on the way - willing me on, and as I drove, Fury took full form.

Entering the cottage, I knew I had been here before, under the behest of Anger, ready to do its bidding. The allegiance earlier in the day had provided assurance, but now the thought of more victims multiplied my madness, and remembering Brett's presence at lunch reinforced my wrath. What was made minuscule and camouflaged by the presence of my children became monstrous in my mere company.

Windows rattled, and a windstorm was on the way. My dear daughters were, thank goodness, flying well ahead of it.

My body felt like it was being battered, and my mind was manic. I thought about my sister being made to do Brett's sinister bidding and the stress she had lived with since. I thought about Jennifer, her childhood crumbling and the cruelty that was still being inflicted. I thought about him sliding in beside my daughters and began drowning in disgust. He talked to them, taunting me by trying to be nice.

His evilness enraged me, and Anger demanded action. What if he had done this to my daughters? Would I not look to exact revenge? Would I not dedicate myself to his demise? Then why was I not willing to do the same for myself and the other martyrs?

It was still early; I could call him at my Aunt's. I could sneak in undercover through a conversation about cows and then, when he was comfortable, attack him with the charges. It worked for the Greeks to capture Troy, so it would surely help me take down this tyrant.

There I was again, right there on the ledge, about to take the leap. The lunge forward earlier in the day helped build a bridge. This bound, though, felt more like a burning. It was intense and insisting on an immediate invasion. I was to show no mercy and smash down the statues of this despot. Civilian casualties, it argued, were an acceptable cost for recompense.

This last command crossed the line of clarity. With it, I began being flung around in a cyclone of confusion. I was being hit by the ache to hurt others and then held close by Hope and Forgiveness. I was being dragged along by my brutality and bloodlust, then rescued by the presence of Patience. I was soothed by lullabies, then tossed into outrage, spurred on by snare drums sounding the steps to war. My throat ached from yelling into the void, and then I heard the whisper of Understanding bearing witness. I was being spun around by self-righteousness, then settled by the strength of Love. But just when I felt safe, I would be snatched again and tossed into the torment. Around I went until I fell to the ground; a dusty wooden floor and a flow of tears were my final saviours.

Crumpled and crushed, I heard the call of the cooking sherry dad had in the cupboard. It had been sitting silently, waiting until I was weak. Now, it was shouting sinister promises. I deserved a drink. Why would I deny myself peace? No one was here to know, and it would be a simple, one-time solution. I could not tell whether my craving was for this alcohol or something that offered true comfort; all I knew was that I was terribly tempted.

"Please, Angel. Help me."

I held no hope, assuming Angel would choose to avoid an Anger hellbent on annihilation.

And yet he appeared.

Chapter 9

No incense was needed for this entrance. An aura appeared first, a halo in human form. A silhouette sprang forth; a sketch in shades of browns, blues and bronze. With further depth and dimension, Angel's shape turned solid and sat beside me. His movements were smooth, unchallenged by his armour. His body effortlessly met my own, in what felt more like a merging. Angel's arms embraced my humanity, and his wings wrapped around my weakness.

My face fell into the softness of his shirt, and I tainted it with tears. His ease showed he did not see these stains as a stigma but as essential. There was no summons to stop; my sobbing simply met with serene strength. My hands searched for something solid to hold onto and met the hard warmth of his armour. The scent of lavender floated around the scene, bringing steadiness and serenity. With the easing of my extreme emotions came the fragrance of rose. It was the precise perfume my mother wore regularly, and which I swore I smelt on several random occasions. It told of support and of care, and came with great comfort.

As the gale battering the glass died down, so did my distress. Mindless mayhem moved into a murkiness, and I waited and worried as to whether it was over; was I simply in the eye of the storm, or had I made it out the other side?

Regardless, I had the space to seek counsel.

"Angel, this is useless. I feel like the only way I can be free is to do something, to lash out and let him have it."

I heard his voice but also felt the reverberations through his chest, the latter resonating with a perfect power.

"I know you seek Freedom, Juno. But Freedom to do what?"

I let this question sink in. Many breaths were taken while I let it bury itself inside and seek an answer grounded in integrity.

Because Angel had chosen his words carefully. He had not asked what I sought Freedom from. The list of what I longed to leave behind was long and well-known: Secret, Shame, Anger, Frustration, Fear, Regret, and the continual call of Revenge. I yearned to be liberated from these things that made me feel flawed and like I was under a force other than my own.

It may have been both impudent and improper, but I had predicted that my burdens would also disappear with dad's death; that Secret and its supporters would dissolve into whatever darkness had spawned them, never to be seen again. But the pain remained present, even with his passing. Dad's presence had been replaced with space, but Secret still found a way to exist within it.

No, Angel was not asking what I sought Freedom from but what I would do when I found it. He was not longing to know the things I wanted to let go of but what I wished to move towards. He prompted me to present a different perspective, not the picture of what was holding me down, but what I was hoping for. He was asking me to reveal what I wanted to be with these wounds.

"Angel, I want the Freedom to give all of me, to live fully, not to forget but to feel. I want to choose courage instead of contempt. I want to be free to get on with my life rather than continually being challenged to "get over it". I want to be free to forge a new future, unrestricted and not continually pushed down by my past. I don't want to spend any more energy wondering what may have been or wasting any more time dreaming of how it could be different.

I want the Freedom to love every experience and let them be.

I want to be free to love me. All of me. And I want the Freedom to love all those around me fully."

My needs were laid out, named and naked.

Angel placed his strong and steady hand on my head, holding and honouring my honesty.

"My Darling, Juno. This is a freedom you already have.

You may be expecting it to make a dramatic entrance or as a seismic shift, but it comes to you in a series of small steps. You construct your Freedom through continuous, common choices. Every day, you decide whether to concede your creative ability to Fear or grab its hand and introduce it to Love.

Freedom is not a magical manifestation, not something I or anyone else can make happen for you. It does not appear through asking but by action. It is an independent duty, a daily dedicated discipline. It requires you to be always alert and eternally evaluating what is truly important. Freedom does not mean an absence of regard but having the ability to choose responses grounded in compassion. Freedom is not a place, but a practice.

And the fullness you seek is forged from finding Love everywhere, even in those things you see as evil."

Anger was still standing between us, looming large. His upper body was ablaze, ready for battle.

Angel lifted his head and looked him in the eye.

"Juno, there is little difference between me and Anger. We are both messengers. But we are not here to make you act mindlessly. Only you hold the wisdom of how we fit into the whole. Truly listen and seek to understand so that we can take our rightful place.

The Secret and Shame that you wish to silence are also saying something. You might not like what they have to say, but have you let them tell their story. Without a voice, you became a victim and were enveloped in silence and violence. But now, can you see, you are imposing the same treatment on these invisible dependents.

You are so intent on imposing your own way and commanding them to comply. Juno, no one likes to be controlled. They would prefer to be cared for.

You have assumed these things seared into your heart are squatters, concerned only with taking possession of your precious property. Have you considered instead, they may be refugees seeking shelter and asking you to secure their safe passage?

Accepting only comfortable messengers will lead to confusion. Trying to cast them away leads to conflict. Turning your back on those hoping for your help is heartless.

To live fully, you need to find the courage to care for all of us, just like you would for each of your children. For we are also your creations."

Angel's pause gave me time to process what felt like a magical mix of the heartbreaking and heavenly.

I had been taught that my emotions were enemies and must be exorcised at all costs. Yet here was Angel presenting an alternative persona; they were not inherently malicious but were a means to understanding. And that living completely, wholly, and authentically required that none are rejected but all are respected. For every feeling comes from your truth, and to deny any the space to speak is a sabotage of the self.

I was reminded of the time, only a year or so ago, when I found out my youngest was cutting herself. I wondered why her lower body was always draped in a blanket, even on the hottest of days. Then, one day, a slip revealed flesh full of slashes, some already shiny scars. The shock cast me into a silent retreat, my thoughts too busy to be turned to speech. The next day, I confronted her with a choice. She would either have to chat with a counsellor, or I would admit her to a private psychiatric facility. She resisted the former but saw it as the lesser effort. After one hour in a closed conversation with the counsellor, my daughter declared it was "all good", and the counsellor said she "had it under control." They were both certain that no further sessions were necessary. I was not so easily convinced.

Further research confirmed that this self-mutilation was a trend, a socially accepted treatment for uncomfortable emotions. Carving, slicing and scarring were standard behaviours. Self-harm had become the tool used to express their hurt and their flesh, the canvas on which they displayed their confusion.

I was at a loss until I read a book that touched on unconditional love. It provided me with an example that I adapted for my own actions. Sitting beside her on the bed, I shared this precious phrase.

"Darling, I will love you if you stop cutting. And I will love you if you continue to cut. It is just that the love will look a little different."

With these words, her acceptance was automatic. There were no exceptions or required exchanges. I was not condoning her harmful choices, but I loved her completely. She was informed that if I did take action, it was out of care and not contempt.

A few weeks later, she came to sit beside me and asked for help with her scars. We discussed the situation openly, and she showed me her thighs. I kept my sigh small, but inside, I was screaming. My poor girl, how badly must she have been feeling to do this to herself. And how much had I been distracted not to discover this earlier? But this was not about me. Besides, any attempt at self-flagellation was futile and only another form of double-dealing. How could I counsel my daughter to care for herself when I was so willing to cover myself in condemnation?

We discussed where she was at and she told me, sincerely, she had stopped. Now she just wanted the scars gone, and in time for summer so she could swim with her friends. It really did feel like a miracle. The grey clouds started to glow, and the sun peeked through the edges. When she knew there was no judgment for her whole, messy self, she could let her guard down, and this came with a new level of confidence and cheer. I had given her a gift, the permission to love the bits of herself she didn't like.

Now, I was being called to do the same for myself.

What came next for my daughter, though, was one of the hardest life lessons, and one that I wished I could have spared her from. However, wisdom is better gained now than later.

The doctor we found to treat her scars said it would take months and a lot of money to make them disappear. There was no overnight option, just a systematic and extremely expensive investment. Her distress was even more heartbreaking than seeing the scars. She learnt then that the hurt you cause yourself has a hangover period. The harm is relatively easy, the healing, much harder.

I knew this road and was so saddened that my daughter would now also have to traverse it. My abstinence from alcohol was only the beginning of the work I had to do to care for my internal wounds. And yet, without a commitment to discovering the cause, the chaos would continue, just in different configurations.

"Juno, where there is Freedom, there is also Responsibility. Just like Secret and Shame, they are intertwined. One cannot act as they wish without some accountability. With the Freedom to love all of you, what would you be responsible to?"

Angel was right; without guidance and grounding, self-determination could swiftly turn to sadism.

First, I would be responsible to my family. Parenthood came with so many promises, although I knew what absconding from these looked like and the damage my avoidance had done. As a provider and role model, it was reckless to maintain the rage and allow bitterness to infuse all my future interactions. I had a responsibility to my family to fill our home with safety and to show what Love does.

To dignify this duty, though, I also had to be responsible for my own person, my potential and the purpose presented – to pass Love on. I was responsible for making my commitment to these things real.

With thoughts of Freedom, my heart had been flying. Now, Responsibility was signalling a safe place to land and for me to step into my power.

"Juno, there is a simple truth. The fact is you were a child. A child who was taught to do what you were told and to obey authority. In this case, authority was used for advantage and to afflict others with the owner's agony. You are not responsible for the actions of others. You are only responsible for your response.

I am sorry, Juno. I am sorry I could not save you from suffering when you were small. I am so sorry I could not magic away the many years of torment. Without them, though, you would not have found your truth. Yes, your pendulum was pushed to the extreme end of pain, but please see the potential it has created. There is a chance now for you to let go and use the momentum for a meaningful swing to peace. "

Angel sat back so he could engage my eyes.

"Juno, I am sorry for so much. But I am not sorry for the person I see now. And I am not sorry that you can finally see me."

"Please tell me, Angel. What do you see?"

"I see a woman who has met many demons. She has spent her life testing ways to triumph over them and wears the scars of many failed attempts. I see someone who is coming into the light of consciousness and beginning to have a real regard for the consequential lessons. I see someone who has gained wisdom from their wounds and is now ready to work with them on what is truly important.

I see someone at the edge of a new world, ready to walk ahead.

And I see that your father is proud of you, Juno."

As Angel spoke, I could picture myself with wings like his own, flying with Freedom, landing with Responsibility and having Love waiting for me to show the way forward.

This image was the inverse of the one I had held within, of a woman who was lost in a land of burning coals, wearing the punishment for being wilfully wicked and a disrespectful daughter.

"But Angel, my cousin's behaviour is stabbing at my heart. At lunch he was so ruthless."

"Juno, were they actually acts of brutality or of remediation? Did they speak of heartlessness or remorse?"

With this, Angel had challenged my singular, dark judgement with an opposing and optimistic interpretation.

I had to smile. I repeatedly and expertly used this universal law to enrage my ex-husband. Every time he would espouse a view, I would show how the contrary could also be true. Now Angel was using the tool I had manipulated to make myself superior, to help me see sense.

"Juno, do you remember when you were just out of rehab. You had caused so much destruction and thrown away trust like it was a trivial piece of trash. It took so many little steps and a continual commitment to restore the relationships you treasured. It took an immense investment from both sides before you could once again be seen as sincere. Every day, you were hauling the heaviness of the harm you caused, and yet you also held hope that maybe the next thing you did would help the healing. If your family had continued to assume your actions were fraudulent, your life would never have been reframed. Where you are now is not just because of your solo struggle. It was also aided by your family's courage and generous goodwill. They were so brave to allow themselves to be vulnerable again, to accept you along with the risk of relapse. They forgave you, Juno. They allowed themselves to again find Faith, and their fortitude has helped build your future.

Yes, your cousin could have been using the situation to usurp your power. But you don't actually know if he was actually seeking forgiveness, because you never afforded him the chance.

Nor have you allowed yourself amnesty."

Angel looked down momentarily, seeming to seek assurance from an internal and invisible source.

"If it is of any assistance, Juno, I do understand how excruciating this endeavour is. The armour you see now is not what I have put on, but what I am still yet to take off. I too am still learning to live with Love, and my transgressions still taunt me. I leave these pieces on not to weigh me down, or to protect my wounds, but to remind me of the strength I have within, of what is possible."

Angel's practice made perfect sense to me, and the symbology resonated within. It was exactly the same reason that I surrounded myself with Buddha statues. They were not there for worship but to remind me of my own wisdom and to practice self-compassion. It was then I became aware of another devious double standard. How ready I was to rely on Memory for moral support, using it to prop me up when I was struggling. And yet, I was so swift to scold it when it would not bend to my whim. No wonder this faculty was erratic; it had merely taken on the character of its master.

"Juno, as long as you consider yourself faulty, you will never find Freedom; you will never take flight.

Where there is a lack of forgiveness for yourself, there will also be fury at others. The punishment you perceive as purposeful will continue to corrupt all your connections.

And as long as you disrespect your experiences, you will never live with Responsibility. All you will do is create more room for Regret.

You are worthy, Juno. You are worthy of health and happiness. And Love longs to be with you."

With these words, Angel held me close and covered me with his cloak.

There was stillness. Silence.

As I fell asleep, I heard him whisper,

"I'm sorry, Juno."

I'M SORRY JUNO

Chapter 10

It was a slow, spiralling process out of sleep, stopping along the way to reconstruct dreams and remember the events of the night before. I was sure I had fallen asleep in Angel's arms, yet here I was in bed. Either I was too exhausted to notice Angel's aid, or his transport was enchanted and effortless. Regardless of the route, I was so grateful to be resting in bed. A few deep breaths brought me more fully awake, and my attention was drawn to a large brown moth on the wall. It was not drab but brilliant, with its wings and body embossed in bronze. I gave it a smile and sat staring at it for a brief time, then suddenly remembered what was required of me.

I ran to the kitchen, poured the cooking sherry down the sink, and put the drained bottle in a garbage bag. I was on kitchen duty today, so it would soon be hidden amongst all manner of partially full jars, open packets and out-of-date condiments. Even though my sister seemed to support my statement that I was solid, seeing this empty bottle would instantly plant seeds of doubt. No, I would spare her this distress and counsel myself with care instead of cruelty for this momentary craving.

By the time I had returned to the bedroom, the moth had gone. I longed to learn more about Angel's life and the ordeals his armour helped him remember. I wondered whether he would ever reveal his sorrows or whether such sharing would be seen as selfish for sentinels.

It was still early, and opening the curtains revealed only clouds and a burst of brisk air. It was refreshing and whispered permission to return to bed. I made a cup of tea, checked the text from my eldest confirming their arrival home and took the chance to snuggle back into the sheets. As my body settled and was still, my mind turned to the extraordinary events of the past few days, processing them and their implications.

I noticed the silence, which felt new and weird. When dad was here, there was always noise. The radio in the lounge came on the moment he was out of bed, creating a constant background buzz of talking and tunes. It was only turned off when the television came on for the night. Then, once the TV was off, the radio beside the bed went on, offering company for the hours in between.

I could feel the battle brewing between being and doing. Through many hard lessons in my childhood, I had learned that lack of activity was laziness, and that sloth was the greatest sin. This was reinforced with vigour during my time as a consultant, where a stacked diary was associated with a sense of self-worth. So, I knew that soon enough, doing would dominate, so I distracted it while I could with my sketchbook and coloured pencils, my constant travelling companions. I started with nothing specific in mind, just playing with some small patterns in the centre. This tiny temple of tangles wandered outwards, and when they did, the inspiration was instantaneous. My etching evolved into a mandala. A very amateur and imperfect one, but a mandala all the same.

My circles were far from flawless, and it took an effort to look past this. This was the reality, though, when you were not working with one already printed or copying from a template. Yet they were as a circle should be simple and complete. Looking at their imperfection took me straight back to primary school, where I was in constant conflict with one of the nuns for being unable to draw a straight line. Even with the aid of a ruler, mine were always a bit wobbly or askew. Sometimes, the top of my finger would sit over the side of the ruler, and be traced into the resulting line, leaving a little bump. My inability to make straight lines was publicly and proudly declared a fault, one that must be rectified if I were to become worthy. While the eyes of those who had decided I was evil were upon me, I worked hard to correct this wrongness. But secretly, I relished it when the ruler slipped, my "sorry", sounding genuine but staying superficial.

Little lines became a big battle until my favourite teacher decided a drawing lesson out on the oval was in order. We went to the edge of the field with clipboards and crayons and spent time sketching the trees. The boy beside me was flustered that he couldn't get his trunk straight. He rubbed out repeatedly and left messy smudges until he ripped up that version and started again. I could appreciate his angst. Mine manifesting more in hesitation, though, than rebellion. At least he had started something.

Seeing this boy's frustration, the teacher got us all to stop. And look. Really look.

"See," she said. "There are no straight lines in nature."

Some boys considered her statement as a challenge, seeking out sticks and inspecting each one closely. Despite them auditing over a dozen, not one was without some kind of curve, crook, knot, or kink. Some lovely little bumps were just like those formed when my finger got in front of the ruler.

With that observation, a huge weight was taken off my shoulders. I was no longer useless; I was a child of nature. While the nuns could express their frustration, I had just found a more meaningful example, a generous judge and a greater justification. I would continue playing their game but knew it was a preference not supported in reality. This was such a simple lesson and yet it had a profound impact. I found it again later in life when I investigated the ancient art of alchemy and came across the quote from an early influential female. She had said, "Look to nature and you will get the answers you seek." I almost heard my teacher's voice read these words as they shared the same wisdom.

I worked on the middle of the mandala first, and it formed into an interpretation of what Angel had seen in me. It was a contrasting combination of sharps and smooths, lights and darks, closed-in colours and open spaces. The incongruous were interconnected and integrated. Each shape existed independently but was also interwoven with its opposite. The homes of Secret and Shame were there, along with Gratitude, Anger, Acceptance, Hate and Hope. This centre felt like the cyclone, a concentration of decades of dramatic conflict.

There was a circle enclosing this one that was concerned, close, yet accepting and compassionate. It did not seek to force the inner form but act as a filter for what would flow outward. It held no ornamentation, no designs or decorations. It was magical in its simplicity, needing to say no more.

Each ring that followed became an investigation into the integration of Freedom and Responsibility and the purpose for which they both were to be employed. With each shape came a conscious consideration of how my independence and accountability could be enacted. One layer honoured my ancestors and their struggles and the next looked into the commitments I made to myself. My children were represented by a bright and beautiful ring, with the preceding circles nurturing and supporting their authenticity. With every single stroke, I could sense the strength that came from the ability to choose, selecting the colours that could either enhance or corrupt what was within the circle.

A large outer layer captured what I could give and receive from the community around me. It confirmed that I should contribute more of my gifts, time and energy. The widest one was a tribute to the world that sustained me and came with a heartfelt contract to care for it.

While the mandala was designed proceeding outwards, I recognised with each layer the mutuality of cause and effect. Unlike the ripples spreading outward from the ducks on the pond, this was an influence in reverse. Yes, I could impact upon ever-increasing spheres, but each concentric context also contributed to my own construction. The extent of interchange, integration and inspiration, though, depended solely on how porous my inner world was. I had been so afraid of all that I was that I had locked myself down lest anything bad escaped. I had made my heart impervious, which successfully stopped scary things from getting out but also prevented all my sparkly parts from providing light to others.

Right on cue, the sun slipped from behind the clouds, certifying all I had just concluded. It also signalled that it was time to start the day. I got up, made breakfast and, feeling a little lonely, put the news on for some company. These wars I watched from afar were real and not just wrought from within. I knew how hard it was to reconcile my own head and heart. I could not comprehend how horrible it would be to have your life and that of your family become wedged between the will of two external warlords. I knew the grief of losing a loved one in a time of peace. I could never genuinely appreciate the depth of despair that comes with clawing your children's crushed bodies out of the collapsed cement you once called home.

I called my eldest, so grateful when she answered. They were just on their way to school, albeit reluctantly. She sounded tired and in desperate need of a sleep in. I reminded her I would return in a few days, and we could have some lovely long slumbers on the weekend. Grandma had promised to take them for ice cream after school. The thought of this treat would see her through. I left the eldest with an, "I love you," and made a mental note to organise some flowers for Grandma. She truly had a generous heart. I had a quick chat with the youngest, who yawned, "Hello", and then asked how I was. She said, "I miss you, Mama", and I could tell she was feeling sad. Right then I felt really bad that I had sent them home so early. I had made the choice for them of continuance, of moving on with the mundane. Perhaps what they really needed was to be part of this disjointed, distressing process. In my concern for their school commitments, I had not considered that more of their healing may have needed to happen here. Instead of solidity and structure, maybe they needed to experience the uneasy and ephemeral.

Hanging up, I let Hurt sit with me. Historically, I would have shoved it aside, noticing it but then choosing to ignore it. Now, I let it be and listened to it for a moment. It told me a tale of desperate love, one wishing to protect my children from any pain. Then, it presented the reality that this was just impossible and showed me the situations in which my choices had been the cause of their challenges. It described itself as living in the dark void between what I wanted and what was real, hanging onto each side, growing to whatever size was needed to fill the gap. It told me that I had isolated myself on one side and not even tried to connect with those on the other side of the chasm. In my attempt to shelter them from suffering, I only caused more separation. If I had involved them in choosing what was important, Hurt may have been smaller and shared. Regret came and sat beside Hurt. Responsibility appeared, holding them tightly and kissing each of their foreheads. Before me, I saw them care for each other and co-exist, and I felt complete.

They stayed as I started the cleanup, chatting with each other and covering many topics. As my attention was absorbed elsewhere, they slowly disappeared. There was no drama, just a dispersion.

The garbage bag began to fill, blanketing the bottle and allowing me to breathe a little easier. There was the same jar of vegemite I had joked with dad about on a visit a year ago. Its expiry date was showing two years earlier, and I had gone to throw it out at the time, alerting dad to my deed. He took it from me, unscrewed the lid and showed me the contents. They looked pristine, the black goo still solid and spotless. He presented the possibility that with all the preservatives, this thing would outlast the cockroaches, and he was probably right. Now, though, it had lost its champion, so in the bag it went. It was followed by a range of chutneys and home-made jams, all harking from a different generation; one where things were made, not bought, and food came from the home and not the shops.

I pictured dad enjoying these on toast with thick butter. Worries about waistlines came second to what he considered delicious. I thought about the freedom this seemed to create, in contrast to the in-laws whose strict diet led to continual self-denial. Even fruit became a source of self-flagellation with days of discipline needed after any enjoyment. I wondered how much effort went into restraining thoughts about food or weighing up the risks and rewards of gratification. Then I wondered whether dad ever felt guilty after his gluttony.

There was a half-eaten box of crackers; something so simple held so many memories. Every night, dad would take his tablets with cheese and crackers to prevent the medication from causing nausea. It was a routine that seemed trivial on my last visit but was now greatly missed.

Grief was there beside me as I put the box in the bag, weighing me down and asking, "why?"

It was late morning when my brother arrived for a trip to the op shop. I was still boxing up the crockery and bric-a-brac, but there were plenty of bags in the bedrooms from the day before. My brother looked weary and worn. While he had taken a few days off work, from his words, I could tell that not being there made him worry. His business was both a blessing and a burden. He was his father's son, and it was hard to break time-honoured habits. I had read somewhere that it is our parents who are the hardest to be unfaithful to, and in this moment, it all made sense.

I dared not engage him with any enquiries about what he knew of Secret. He was too young to have known what was going on for me and would have been well-supervised elsewhere when she came into being. I only hoped he did not remember the role plays I revised with him when we were alone. And wished I did not either. Why would Memory cover over the cruel conduct of others yet openly advertise my own atrocities? Or was it only doing the will of its master? I knew Angel had confirmed that I was a child and was only doing what I had been taught. I wondered if there would ever be a part of me that would come to believe that.

Shame popped up, showing me its sadistic smile, revelling in my propensity to take far more than my share of responsibility. Respect came to stand in front, frustrating Shame's efforts to be the foremost force. Respect shed light on lessons learned, my brother's own pain, the preciousness of parenthood, and the opportunity that was being offered at that moment.

So, my brother and I talked about the weather, how it had turned, and reminisced about the crazy Christmas when it had snowed; a shock given it was in the middle of summer. It would be Christmas again soon, with this year's not likely to bring snow but guaranteed to bring sadness. I told my brother the girls thought I was crazy because I didn't want to put up decorations this year. The eldest had told me in a silly, sarcastic tone that she was shocked and disgusted and that I should go to the mirror and take a good, long, hard look at myself. How right she was. If I did that now, I would be sure to see some of my mother there and be compelled to pass on some of her passion. At the time, though, I told her they were welcome to light the place up. I just had no energy left for commercial exploitation or such transient excitement. I made a mental note to reconsider my decision on the plane trip home. It would be a wonderful way to honour Poppy in our own home.

I know people were suspicious about the hate I held for Christmas; as if I played Grinch just to goad others, or as an attention-seeking strategy. Yet I was in no doubt of the size and sincerity of the distaste I held for this day. It was my birthday, but it was never a day I associated with delight, only disappointments. I remember being told that the doctor had given mum some medication to try and postpone my birth so that he could have Christmas away from the hospital and with his family. I came anyway, delivered by the doctor in a Santa Suit (or so I imagined). Was my entrance into this world then considered inspirational or merely an inconvenience? Was the fact that I was not a son also a source of sadness?

A big deal was always made about Christmas, with the mornings spent opening presents from Santy and preparing the forthcoming feast. My birthday came later in the afternoon when everyone was too full, tired, and hot to be excited about cake. Mum offered to have a party for me on another day, but it did not feel the same. It was not sincerely mine. The result is that I had grown up always feeling like my birthday came second-best. Or was this just another story I had pieced together from particular parts? Angel had prompted me to consider that there was always another perspective.

I clearly remembered, though, the day my Christmas Spirit died. I was in town with mum, in the motorbike shop, buying a helmet for my brother. I was hanging behind when I heard her say to the salesman, "We have to get something from Santy, don't we?" At that moment, all the magic surrounding the invisible man melted away, and I was dumped into a drab world of deceit. I had always sensed that the Santa Clauses in the shopping centres were scams. There was no way I would ever let them hold me, and my screams showed how scary I thought they were. They could not be real because Santy was heavenly and kind, pure and compassionate, and so could never evoke that much terror. I had based the beauty of Christmas on the belief that something or someone miraculous was involved, and this was now mangled.

I did not know what was worse, that Santy did not exist, or that my parents had lied to me all this time. After I opened my Santy present that year, I ran to the room crying. I could not hold the agony in any longer. My parents initially thought I was being a spoilt brat, not liking the little jewellery box with the dancing ballerina. They seemed much less concerned when I told them it was because the gift was not from Santy. This stupidity was something I would get over and unlike pretentiousness, my naiveté did not need punishment.

When my time came to choose an approach to Christmas for my family, I could feel every fibre of my conscience being twisted. Despite my past distress, I was compelled to play the game with my girls. I heard on television that supporting the Santy story helps with imagination, so I grabbed onto this justification to join the crowd. Besides, it did brighten their days, and I could not begin to think of the horror at school if I sent them in saying Santy did not exist. Although I sure thought about it at times, and it certainly made me smile. This conflict made me appreciate the strange mix of statements and questions that my mother made in the motorbike shop that day. Part of her sounded so sure that this was the proper path, the other seeking support for a practice she may have thought shonky. I wondered if she was around whether I would have asked her for advice about my angst, or whether raising my doubts would have been viewed as disrespectful to her decisions.

Over cake and coffee, I thanked my brother again for the girls' adventure on his bike and apologised if my eldest's enthusiastic engagement with him on social media crossed the line from support to stalking. He smiled and said it was "all good". I got the sense that he actually adored the attention. I did not want to ask whether he and his girlfriend were trying for children. It seemed like such a simple question, but I knew how many layers of longing were burrowed beneath the surface. I understood the unstated expectations and how dealing with them involved investigating your own identity. We had not evolved far from a time when your ability to reproduce was seen as a sign of success and a source of self-worth. This was not the time to raise these torments. There were many other this man was dealing with.

We confirmed the details for the meeting with the solicitor later that day. We would sit and read dad's will and have the chance to discuss the next steps. My brother said he would rather not go because it felt like gold-digging. I did agree, but suggested that the formality also afforded us the chance to conclude the clerical crap. "I guess so", was followed by a quick hug, and then he left. Back inside, with many bags and boxes gone, it was already starting to feel empty. It was as if this home was being hollowed out, all traces of personality being removed and restored to tabula rasa. The immediacy of this action almost felt like an invalidation. It seemed to declare a disrespect for the decades over which these items were collected and cared for and the life that loved them. It was important, though, that I helped with the heavy lifting while I was here, and it did provide opportunities for us to connect, even if it was only over old photographs, chipped plates and broken belts.

I didn't see my sister that morning. I suspected she was busy organising property sales and arranging auctioneers. There were also lots of authorities to advise and bills to pay. The administration of a life and its legacy was arduous, and it was sad that someone's passing was sullied with paperwork. My eldest and I once talked about how I would like to be sent off. I told her my only criterion was that the form it took must be low-cost and legal. I think these kinds of options are limited. And even if I had the chance to fulfil my desire to go out with a flaming, floating Viking funeral, there would still be forms to fill out afterwards. Perhaps the kids would need a fire permit as well. My wish then, is to die in winter.

Maybe my sister also needed some space to process the past few days and contemplate the transition that she was in. After mum had died, she turned her attention to dad, and while there were times of terrific tension, she had been present through all of his troubles. I wondered whether the void would be valued or seen as a problem to be resolved. It was only a day, too, since she found out we shared a shameful secret, and if she was anything like me, this is not something you simply brush away.

My thoughts took a back seat as I pulled bags from the pantry covered in cockroach casings. The crunchy shells were in every crevice. Right then, I wished I had worn gloves, but it was too late. Despite the initial disgust, I did admire these creatures. They had one simple priority and sole standard for success – survival. Or at least that was the stereotype I had assimilated. Regardless of the accuracy of this portrayal, I was now responsible for eradicating every trace of their existence from these cupboards. Suddenly, I was captured by how closely this process resembled my path forward. I could clean away the mess the cockroaches had made, but they would simply be waiting elsewhere; there was no closure. Their numbers may dwindle, but they would never be definitely destroyed. I either needed to reconcile to this reality, accept it, and be comfortable with continued contribution to cleanliness, or commit myself to eternal vigilance and violent means of extermination. I could see the pros and cons of each approach, but only one offered the chance of peace.

After dealing with the cockroach dilemma, I added dad's rifles to the list of to-dos. There was one pellet shooter he used to scare off starlings in the shed and one that used bullets when he needed a bigger burst of bravery. I remembered him boasting on the phone one Sunday night that he had successfully assassinated the annoying Koel bird that was keeping him awake. The pellet rifle was the source of so much fun when the girls and I were last here. Dad loaded them up, and they took turns trying to hit a cardboard target. The challenge created a beautiful collaboration, and I stood back to witness them work together. There was a rise in regard for their grandfather as the girls sensed the skills needed to shoot. And a profound respect was granted when they were given the responsibility of a rifle. I could see how it was much more than just handing over a gun; with it came a tendering of trust. How this was used could either build a bond or break it apart. Beneath this tangible transaction, there were innumerable invisible interactions.

I had felt the importance of these when dad took me to the rifle range once when I was in high school. He enjoyed shooting in competitions and the camaraderie that came with being part of a club. He felt so bad when I ended up with a big bruise on my cheek because I was not ready for the recoil.

We laughed about it later, but back then, I was really worried something was broken. This anxiety was nothing compared to the pain dad felt when he had to use his skill to kill one of his cows, when slaughter was a preferable alternative to suffering. For dad, killing, even with the intention of kindness, was cruel.

This reflection came with tremendous remorse. How many times through my addiction had dad handed me his heart, and how many times had I torn it and trashed it. How many times had my family offered me hope, and how many times had I stolen it and smashed it. But they kept coming back with a belief that was much bigger and braver than mine. Sadness was there, sitting with the sins of the past. Pity and Pride had hands elevated, eager to be the next emotion embraced. But Freedom and Responsibility came into the foreground, muting the manic pair. Pity and Pride would have to wait.

I returned to the task at hand: sorting, stacking, bagging, wrapping, and boxing. Without the hourly reminders from the radio, I had lost track of time and did not rest from this rhythm until mid-afternoon. I chowed down some cake (mentally committing to eating some vegetables for dinner), made a take-away coffee, put what I could in the car, and took off to make a quick delivery before the meeting.

At the op shop I saw the pile of dad's possessions my brother had deposited earlier. The volunteers were working their way through them, preparing them for sending elsewhere or selling in their shop. I thought about where they may end up. They may form part of a young family's first home and be with them through meals for many years. They may end up in a communal office kitchen and keep people company through lonely lunch breaks. Or they may be claimed by the charity and used to serve health and hope to the homeless. Dad's suits may be bought by one nervously awaiting an interview or a first date, knowing the outcome could define their future. Or they may be snapped up by a student and used as a source of amusement at a dress-up party. It disappointed me to think that something in which dad took such pride may be used as a plaything. Although dad loved a laugh, it so it may be a fitting finale for these clothes. Wherever these whisps of dad's energy went, I wished them well.

Compared to the marvellous mix of merchandise at the op shop, the solicitor's office was simple and sedate. It smelt vaguely of disinfectant spray and sounded like suspense. In the waiting room, my sister sat wearily, watching the walls. My brother sullenly scrolled through supplier stock lists, preparing an order for parts. When he was done, we shared status updates, and I sought their advice about the firearms and ammunition. My sister suggested I pop into the police station after the meeting, which sounded like a very sensible strategy. My sister had arranged for the real estate agents to visit tomorrow and the auctioneer's assessment early next week.

When the office door opened, we were welcomed in with the common condolences and confirmations of my father's credibility. "He was a good man", hinted that his time had ended. However, I knew there was much about my father that endured. The solicitor's handshake was sticky from hand sanitiser, with the scent of pure alcohol staining my skin.

"You must be Juno. You are the only one I have not met yet."

My assent almost doubled as an apology for how little I had been involved in dad's affairs. In fairness, no one had ever asked me for help, and I would have given it willingly. But then, if I were to be completely honest, I never asked if they needed assistance or if there was anything I could do. Sure, my sister's previous treatment could be used as justification. Still, I had guarded my generosity. Shame knew it too, going to sit in the spare chair in the corner.

The solicitor handed us each some printed pages, with the set stapled at the top. They started with "The final will and testament" and stopped with dad's signature. Separately, he handed us a spreadsheet. He had been in touch with the accountant and had recorded the existing investments and debts. The spreadsheet showed the sum of what was known now and estimates to account for future sales. He led us into a reading room where we could have some time to digest the details. My sister asked why my aunties were not there. In my preoccupation, I had not even noticed. We were promptly informed that they were not mentioned in the will and, as such, were not invited to attend.

Dad's directions were simple.

All possessions were to be sold, and all investment and savings accounts were to be cleared. The combined proceeds were to be split seven ways: three for the siblings and four for the grandchildren. They were to be even and exact shares, with no favour or weighting. As children and adults, us siblings always argued about the differential in dad's affections, all citing evidence to show some kind of favour. But this will attested to the actual parity with which he worked. He would always give to others what he had given to one. Fear floated by, fleeting but well-formed. Would they think these fractions were fair, given my failures?

The exception to this edict of equality was my childhood home. It would be kept, with the deeds transferred to my sister. I was sincerely happy for her. She had sacrificed so much, and now she had some security. I told her so, too. My "I'm glad for you", was met by my brother saying, "Me too." The support I was able to provide her at that moment created an air of optimism over our ongoing relationship.

The bottom line was that dad had accumulated over $2.4 million in assets. Each person was to be gifted approximately $344,000.

My incredible father. While he enjoyed living only with the essentials, he had prudently piled away the profits from his enterprise. He did the same with the money from mum's estate, adding it to the stash, compounding, and creating a consequential cache.

The immensity of this inheritance was overwhelming. The intense implications induced tears. My brother and I would also be mortgage-free by mid-life. My daughters could pay for their college fees, buy a car and still have enough for a healthy deposit on a house of their own. My father had taken care of all the fixtures of financial freedom. All those years he flogged himself to the bone had been for us and this finish line. The decades of dedication to his work, of physical and emotional exhaustion had culminated in this most caring contribution to the life of his children. All the weight he bore was now lessening ours. The absences that caused so much angst had accumulated this final offering.

Sadness came to stand beside me. For then I realised that while I was busy battling demons of the past, dad was forging a way forward for my future. The world I knew when I walked in had been put up on the shelf, and I now had the tools to build a new one. It was as if a genie had appeared to grant my material wants. Yet all I could think about was how incredibly grateful I felt and the magnitude of my father's generosity. Right then and there, all I wished for was to hug him one last time.

Chapter 11

When I made it back to the cottage I was still in a haze, working through all that had happened at the solicitor's office. Just like the cyclone the night before, there was a contrasting mix of emotions. My heart was breaking for the loss of a man who had given us so much, but it was also bright with the excitement of crafting a new future. The separate sides of my heart sang different songs, yet they did exist together as a duet. These were the voices of Grief and Faith. I could hear Angel telling me that the latter was available to me without the financial freedom, and I could understand that. At the moment, though, I was happy to honour the help that this material gift provided. I sat on dad's bed and looked up in case his spirit was there listening. Through tears, I thanked him, although the words seemed insufficient. I hoped the chorus in the centre of my chest provided a more meaningful message.

I allowed the singers their space and continued cleaning while they perfected their partnership. Once I was comfortable that the cottage was in an acceptable condition for the agents, I downed tools and called the girls. Picking up the phone, I could not help but consider whether my sister would accept my handiwork or have to invest her effort into overcoming my ineptitude. I wondered whether she would go around reworking my efforts to meet her standards of excellence. The thought was almost automatic and definitely habitual, but at that moment, it also felt disrespectful.

The girls were about to have dinner, so we only talked briefly. I held back telling them about the will and what we had received. I wanted the time to pay proper tribute to the toil that had generated this gift and to allow due regard for the opportunities it afforded. So, we shared a quick snapshot of the day and confirmed the details of my arrival the following afternoon.

I had kept one can of soup from the pantry clean-up, so I heated the contents and combined them with some buttery toast. I thought about putting the news on but instead decided to cherish the silence. This time tomorrow would see me back being mum and sharing space with my kids, three dogs, and a cat. I would also return to being a consultant, with deadlines looming for my clients. Simple moments like this then, with an absence of immediate demands and external accountabilities were sparse and incredibly special.

I was unsure whether my home may be conducive to angelic company, and I didn't want to leave without the chance to be with Angel again. So, I asked him to join me. It took less than a minute for the man to manifest, yet it was done purposefully and peacefully. Angel sat opposite me, his wings hanging on each side of the seat. For a moment, I merely enjoyed his presence, not feeling any pressure to push forward. There was an implicit invitation to use this time as I wished. I wanted to ask some questions and understand more about my magical mentor, and so after some simple greetings, I began.

"Angel, are you really with me always?"

"Yes, Juno, I am."

"How does that work though? Are you like an invisible spirit sitting up in the corner of my room?"

"Sometimes, yes. Being with you though is more like the ebb and flow of the ocean. The water is always there, as I am. When I am wanted, I come forward like a wave and when my work is done, I pull back into the energy around you. Or perhaps it is better explained by the breeze you love so much. You are surrounded by air at every moment, and that is my abode. Most of the time you are not even aware of it, until it begins to dance around you. When it is no longer needed, it simply settles back into space."

With this explanation I was assured that Angel did know me. He had sensed my delight when breezes brushed against my body, my joy when it flowed past my face and feet. He knew how meaningful this movement was to me, and his explanation had made it even more so. I thought about how little awareness I brought to my environment, how mostly I simply existed within it. In my state of self-absorption, I had not considered that I was merely one element in a myriad of energies. I made a mental note to spend more time sitting with this and pressed on with my enquiries.

"Do my daughters have an angel like you?"

"Yes, they have their own version that is evolving with them."

That thought lifted a weight off my shoulders. I was not alone in this parenting process. Sitting with Angel, I realised that this assumption was founded on ignorance, arrogance, or a bit of both.

This lofty thought was soon superseded by some lowly logistics.

"OK, but what about when I am undressed? Are you there then? What about when I am on the toilet? Are you watching me poop? Oh my gosh, do you see me when I pick my nose?"

A smile spread across Angel's face, igniting his eyes. Ah, so heavenly spirits did have a sense of humour. I wondered if Angel laughed and logged that as a future challenge.

"If you need me during any of those daily duties, then I am there; not to judge what your body may be doing, but to care for your both your being and your becoming."

"Is there a plan, Angel. I mean, is there a pathway prescribed for me. Is there such thing as Fate, and if so, is it just standing by and watching me flounder towards the finish line?"

"No, Juno. In this life you are fully free. You are only bound by your own beliefs."

Another mental note was made. I needed to articulate my beliefs and focus on the fences defining my future.

"Juno, may I ask you a question?"

I was taken aback by this request, and I was sure the surprise showed. I had come to expect Angel to provide answers. I had not considered that maybe he, too, was still seeking something.

"What do you see in me, Juno?"

I was overwhelmed. Here was a higher being asking my opinion of him, inviting me to share my impressions and insights. Suddenly, I went from being a beneficiary of his blessings to a participant and partner. The shift was significant and, for a moment, unsettling. His longing was not lost on me, nor was the honour I had of now helping him. I needed to nurture Angel. I reached out and took his hand, engaged his entreating eyes and took a few deep breaths. Then I began.

"Angel, I am sorry, for my words will only be simple. They cannot convey the fullness of my feelings. I am limited by language. This is the best way I can describe what I see and sense.

Before me, Angel, I see beauty. Yes, in your bodily form, but also in your very being. I see a manifestation that is magical and feel an aura that is authentic. You are in the true sense of the word – awesome.

In you Angel, I see strength, not showy or superficial, but deep-seated and disciplined. Through you, I have come to appreciate what courage can be. I also see vulnerability, but not one you wear like a wound. Your vulnerability, Angel, feels like a validation of your valour.

I see in you a firm and fundamental faith, not formed from the tenets of others but from facing many tests and trials. Before you came, I could not grasp the concept of Grace. Being held by you has made it real.

Angel, I see someone dancing divinely between heaven and earth and calling me to do the same. In you, I see light, and I see Love. And from you, Angel, I feel Love. With you, Angel, I feel whole."

Before I had finished, tears were gathering in my eyes and in his.

One slipped down his face.

I walked over to his side, sat beside him, and hugged him, a physical attestation of my vast admiration.

Minutes passed in a mutual embrace.

"Juno, you know that you can only see in others what is also within yourself."

That thought brought forth more tears and a tighter hug. I sat holding him, hoping that he understood the depth of my appreciation. I turned my mind to what else I could do to make my point, but I realised that any need for further displays would simply be for my satisfaction, not his. I thought about how nice it was to see Angel smile and decided to follow through on my dare.

"Angel, I also see a man-bird with massive wings. Do you have to sun yourself to prevent parasites?"

I imagined him splayed out on my garden mound like the magpies and the neighbours driving by, dumbfounded. I felt his chest shake and heard him chuckle. Could we be sharing the same silly image? I sat back to see his response and, through the radiance, perceived the pure and profound.

"Can I?", I asked, reaching towards Angel's wings. He nodded his assent.

I stroked the sides of the wings softly. They were as smooth as water but neither slick nor wet. They were as soft as the air but also sturdy as a shield. These wings were a masterful mix of solidity and space. How the individual feathers fitted together was a fantastic feat, faultlessly folded into one another. Each feather would float or fall separately, but together, they affected flight.

I turned my attention and touched the armour on Angel's arm, acknowledging it as an artefact of his own troubles.

"Do you think you will ever take this off?"

"I don't know right now, Juno. It feels good to have it on. But do you think I should let it go?"

"I think its symbology is really important. But is it helping or hindering you become the person you want to be? Is it causing you to hold onto the past or projecting you towards your potential?"

"I am not sure."

"Then you could do an experiment."

With this word, I ceased exploration and embarked on enthusiasm. I always gained immense joy from trying things, testing the waters, and learning realities that can only be gained from giving things a go.

"You could take it off even for a few minutes and feel what arises. Then you will know where you are at and what to do next. Now you are only guessing what it feels like for it be gone. Only by actually removing it and having regard for your response can you understand what is currently unclear."

"That sounds like a wonderful idea. I will. Thank you, Juno."

He opened his wings as an offering, and I wiggled into them. And then I realised that my response was as meaningful for me as it was for Angel.

"Just so you know, Angel, I see what you did there. Very clever, Angel, very clever indeed."

I felt him chuckle again.

The counsel I provided to Angel was exactly the advice I also needed. This consult was delivered with a generosity that I found hard to give myself yet was crucial to the end goal. I contemplated the contrast between how willingly I poured out mercy for this man and withheld this same kindness for myself. I thought about how helping Angel with his dilemmas brought greater regard to my own and made me feel far less alone. I was brought back to one of the basic teachings of Buddhism, the two wings of wisdom and compassion and felt them folded around me.

"Thank you, Angel." Those words were delivered with all that I was, which, right then, did not feel big enough.

I don't know how long I allowed myself to be held because I became hypnotised by Angel's heart. It was less of a beat and more of a tone, less of a throb and more of a blend, a beautiful balance of bass and treble. Its sound sunk into the senses, and it emanated an energy that was entrancing. Cuddled against it, I felt complete.

I awoke the next morning wrapped in sheets instead of wings. There was no moth on the wall, but as I gazed out the window, I heard a cockatoo screech and saw a white feather fall.

I went about the morning feeling heavy but hopeful. The bed that begot Secret was moved to make more space for the boxes and bags from the lounge and kitchen, leaving the latter neat and ready for the agent's arrival. There were repeated entries and exits from Secret's room before I realised the opportunity that I had on this day, and which soon would be gone. The next movements were much more mindful.

I stood outside Secret's room and asked the little girl to join me. She took some time to consider the call, scanning the scene and inspecting the intention of the invitation. I honoured her hesitation, and when she stood beside me, I offered my hand. There was a delay while she decided if I could be trusted, then she took it, and held it tight. We walked together into that room, slow, steady steps signalling the significance. I walked to the one small space left on the bed and sat down. I opened my arms for the little girl, and shyly, she came to sit on my lap. I held her with all that I had.

There were no tears from the little girl, but mine flowed freely.

"Why are you crying?", asked the little girl.

"I am so sad about what happened to you here. I am sorry, Juno. I am so sorry that he hurt you, and I am so sorry that no-one was here to help."

Her tiny arms wrapped around me, and her head leant into my chest.

"It's alright", she said. "You're here now."

My heart tore open. All the scars split wide, and the wounds within saw their first flare of forgiveness. The gentleness they had longed for was granted by this little girl in the gingham dress. The cry that came out of my body was not of pain or protest but of capitulation. I would cede my complex, confused, chaotic country to the simple state of compassion for the sake of this child. She was still here with me; she was precious, and she did not need to witness any more suffering. I would surrender, finally ending the decades-long war. I would make peace with all parts of me and provide a place of peace for this pure spirit.

"There is someone I would like you to meet."

Secret stepped out of the shadows, and the girl promptly pulled back.

"It's OK.", I said, stroking the girl's hair. "This is Secret. She lives with us too. She may seem a little shocking at first, but there is no need to fear her. She has been left alone for so long, but we will take care of her now. Secret came to sit beside us. The child turned to face her and placed her small hand on one of Secret's. Following her lead, I let one of my arms move around Secret's back, supporting her and showing her that she was safe.

"Yes! Don't worry. We will take care of you, Secret." She smiled at this strange guest and snuggled into me once more. Shame was nowhere to be seen, but I knew a time would come when I would need to introduce this innocent to that wraith, and when we would also cover it in warmth.

We waited together in this space, this place, to finally come to know one another and cherish our connection. Our time was interrupted by cars crushing the gravel at the front gate. After a quick kiss on each of their cheeks, the girl and Secret disappeared, and I dashed to the bathroom to wash my face and cool my eyes. When the knock came, it was still clear I had been crying. However, when I met my sister in the lounge room, her eyes were exactly the same.

She introduced me to the agent, who had entered behind her and was already making notes. They both declined beverages, so I left them on their tour and logged in on my laptop. I had no idea how long the lethargy that surrounded me would last, but my clients could not wait. I sent status emails and booked briefings for the Wednesday next week, giving me a few days to get my head around how to make the due dates work with the demands of Grief. The inheritance was invaluable but it did not invalidate my need to earn an income, nor would simply living off it satisfy my Ego.

The agent's audit moved outside, and my sister showed him around the garden, through the sheds, and to the paddocks across the road. At the conclusion, he stood back beside his car, capturing a few more observations while my sister came into the cottage. She said her goodbyes to me at the door.

"We are taking off to see dad's farm now. I won't get to see you before you leave. I will give you a call next week to talk about the way forward. Have a good trip home."

"Thanks," I said, signalling a wave. By the time I got to "take care", she had already turned and started closing the door behind her.

There was little time to reflect on the earlier reunion in the room. Just as my sister left, my brother arrived, bringing some vegetable pastries for lunch. My thanks were met with his explanation.

"I didn't think there would be anything left here to eat, and there is nothing at the airport. Anyway, I hope you like them."

We sat, ate, and discussed the next steps. Out of optimism, I asked how he was and received the standard reply of, "OK."

"Is there anything I can help you with?"

He thought for a moment.

"Yes, there may be. I want to put an article about dad in the local paper, about all the work he did and his contribution to the community. The paper said they would love to have it, but I am not much of a writer. Do you think you might be able to help me with it?"

"That would be wonderful, I would love to. Let's chat about it on the way."

I quickly cleaned up while he packed his van with another load of dad's legacy and put my luggage on top. With him waiting, I said my farewells, uncertain whether these would be final. I went room to room, touched the walls, and blew a kiss, wishing whoever entered well.

As my brother drove, we discussed dad's piece for the paper. He wanted to highlight dad's work on restoring heritage and his inventions that transformed the local industry. I remembered so much of these men's relationship being navigated by Anger. It was nice to see the next stage of its passage being piloted by Pride. I pulled out my notepad, recorded his ideas, and penned my email address on a ripped-off page. I promised I would set up an outline for the article early next week and give him a call to figure out how to flesh out the details.

The drop-off was swift, avoiding the danger of an emotional display. I was early, but happy to wait, looking forward to some time to process all that had happened over the past few days. As I walked towards the gate, I passed by a man and met eyes I knew. It was my first boyfriend. His body and face had aged, but his eyes were still as shiny as those I swooned over as a teenager. Our immature romance had begun in the public park beside the Blue Light Disco when I was introduced to a friend of a friend. I was sixteen, and he would have been just over twenty. I was inspired by his independence, encouraged by his creativity, and comforted by his consideration and care. He wore the black leather of a biker, but beneath his bravado lived a gentle man. Sure, he was a rebel, but a recalcitrant with respect. In that instant, I tried to remember why we broke up. I could not identify any particular instant; however, with my parentage and the age difference, it would have been inevitable.

We stopped beside each other and shared a friendly frown.

"Simon?"

"Yes! Juno?"

"Yes! How wonderful to see you. How are you?"

It seemed like a silly question to ask after thirty years, but still, it stimulated some speech that shuffled into more small talk. He was living in the same city as me, just on the opposite side, and producing music, which I remembered was his passion. He had come home for the funeral of his older brother. I told him of my father, and we exchanged sincere sympathies. I followed my heart and launched into a hug, which was well met.

"It is funny how things work, Simon. I am so glad I got to see you, because I always wanted the chance to say thank you."

The quizzical look on his face coaxed me to continue.

"Mum told me you came to see her when she was sick and that you told her she had a beautiful daughter. Simon, I know she took that to heart, and it gave her great solace. It meant the world to her, and to me."

"And I meant it, Juno."

He held my hand, the small squeeze solidifying his message.

"I have to go now, but let's see if we can chat more on the plane."

Simon sped over to who I assumed were his parents and someone who seemed to be his sister.

I went to the gate and found a seat where I could stare out the window. I sent a text to the girls confirming my location, saying that I was so looking forward to seeing them again and that I loved them. My words were answered with a chain of emojis, expressing their sentiments simply, succinctly, and more successfully than my sentences.

The meeting with Simon made me smile. For so long, I had wanted him to know how much his actions were appreciated, and now that had been achieved. Still, his comments had created a curiosity bordering on concern. Who was the teenage girl he remembered? Was he merely being polite to bring my mother some peace? But he said he had meant it, so how could his Memory of me be so different than my own. Beautiful was certainly not a word I would have used to describe myself. My adjectives would have consisted of pudgy, clumsy, silly and insecure. The girls at school would have added smelly and styleless to the list. Why was I so willing to cling to those views voiced as criticisms and yet so ready to cast away commendations?

There, in the airport I called that teenager forward, and sat with her, not as a parent or a peer but as the woman who had welcomed the child into her arms earlier that day. I looked at her list of achievements and awards. I saw her struggles and the times she succumbed. I watched as she fell and felt how much it hurt. Then, I saw her getting up again and choosing to go on. I saw how those things others judged deficiencies were either unique quirks or useful adaptations to an absurd world. I observed those times when she opted for actions that were horrendously disrespectful and even harmful and how they weighed heavy upon her. I held her hand, as Simon had held mine, as a sign of reassurance and regard for all she had endured and the beauty that still lay beneath.

The conversations I had with this teenager were silent, essential so as not to startle those sitting close. I provided her with explanations, but not excuses, observations and more balanced opinions. As the flight was called, I asked her to come with me and help me with my girls. She was worried about what she had done in the past, but I confirmed that this made her a wise counsel. She accepted, acknowledging that she had many suggestions for how I could support my girls more effectively. She came aboard as my guest and my guide, and I was grateful for both.

I had three intentions for the flight home. The first was to use the time to transition back from daughter and sister to mum, to get my head and heart back into my home. The second was to make a list of what was truly important and, on my return, place it beside my bed. And lastly, I was going to seek out Simon to continue our conversation. I achieved none. I fell asleep shortly after sitting. When I awoke and went to the bathroom, I saw Simon snuggled against the window, using his jacket as a pillow and the time to get some rest. I returned to my seat and to sleep, happy to heed my body's advice for a bit longer.

I was still feeling dulled when we disembarked, but the fog faded when I saw my daughters, their smiles and excitement. The eldest was holding flowers, and from their form, I knew they had made a special trip to our favourite florist. Grandma gave me a bit hug, her tears spilt in solidarity with the sorrow surrounding us. The reunion was reasonably serene; the shroud of loss was still heavy. I was so involved with my daughters that I did not see Simon, but I was not worried. I was sure we would meet again if the time was right. If not, then that simple exchange would surely sustain me.

The ride back home was punctured between pleasantries and peaceful pauses. We talked about plans for dad's possessions and ours for the weekend. My Mother-in-law thanked me for her lovely flowers and the groceries I had delivered for them. I did this whenever they went to stay, saving the grandparents the expense of catering to added appetites and ensuring children and adults had access to special treats. Grandma could not stay for tea; otherwise, Grandpa would throw a tantrum. So, after some very warm entwines, she went on her way.

The welcome from the dogs was wonderful. There was the wild wagging of tails, bouncing of furry bodies and woeful whines of wanting. I gave them attention to ease their ache and then arranged their dinner. Two of the dogs, a brother and sister pair, were old now. Their walk was weary and sometimes they lost all strength in their legs. The collapse would be followed by a look of confusion and continual attempts until ability was regained. I was worried about what the next few months would hold for these friends, but as long as they came running for food, my anxiety was allayed.

All the girls and I could conjure was pizza and trashy TV, but these felt perfect. We enjoyed judging the pretentious princesses prancing around in stilettos and buying stacks of Prada. The show itself was fiction, but we had seen enough on social media to know that for a rare few, this was their reality. The excess and egomania exuding from the screen did not create the right environment to present Poppy's gift. It would only pale against the pink Porsche and Dom Perignon.

When we had enough exuberance, I turned off the TV and told them about my altered view of Christmas adornments. I figured there would be no harm in applying their fashion sense to a functional use. I suggested that this year, we should use the chance to celebrate our ancestors, all of those whose hard work had helped us to be here. And, I had decided, it should be done in a style they deserved. This latter thought lit up their faces and freed their imaginations. I had provided the directions, but they decided the details. They came and cuddled, and we decided the next day would be spent shopping for supplies and printing photos of the people we would honour on our tree. I had resisted taking part in the festive season for so long because I perceived it as a lie. I had been actively antagonistic against something I felt was a falsehood. Only now did I realise how much energy I had spent clinging to this story and shaping it into a justification. This letting go had waited a long time.

Despite my emotional exhaustion, I was overwhelmed with joy to see my bed. While I bad-mouthed materialism and preached the perils of a preoccupation with possessions, I was happy to be hypocritical when it came to my bed. I loved and longed for it, and I told it so each night. I thought about how similar my reaction was to that of my dogs. Instead of wags, though, there were wriggles into the sheets. Instead of whines, there were sighs of satisfaction. Where my hands had proffered pats, they now stroked pillowcases. Grief had been shadowing me all day and it crawled into the other side. But I knew this beloved abode could hold the two of us. I turned to look outside, through the glass deck doors, to a night illuminated by a near-full moon. I spied my special star, the one that saw me off to sleep most nights and moved my hands through moon rays that had come to meet me in my room. I let one linger on my palm while I gave my thanks for the day and sank into sleep.

The next day began with a solo butcher bird sending out a simple yet superb signal. I loved laying here acknowledging its perfection and listening for the next instrument to be layered upon this introduction. Many mornings, I allowed myself the joy of simply being aware of this orchestration, keeping my eyes closed to fully appreciate its elements and evolution. Soon, the magpies joined the lone, lovely voice, adding variety and reverberation. Not to be outdone, the currawongs would push in and add their pure and piercing part, replicating their powerful presence. The kookaburra cackles always sent a smile, although I could not help but wonder whether the laughing was done with or at the audience. The cockatoos would come next, knowing that their screech would surpass the croon of any contender and satisfied just to do the day their way. It took a cacophony of lorikeets to compete with the cockatoo's crude call. The combination of clamour and chatter created a chaotic carnival and a crazy, wonderful welcome to the day.

In the throes of addiction, I hated hearing the bird's morning music. It was an insidious sign of the choices to come. As soon as I allowed myself to awaken, I would be accosted by the alternatives of conceding to my commitments or to my cravings. The tunes that now delivered so much delight, back then beget dread. The prompts that today brought pleasure felt like a punishment. I would try to block them out and banish them from my consciousness. This thought still came with some hurt, of how many years I had spent pushing away real pleasure. I knew that my ability to choose had been compromised and that my brain had been broken, but still, the knowledge that I had succumbed to destruction still stung. However, at this moment, there was something more important than regret. I had reclaimed my power and would use it toward my purpose.

Slowly through this symphony, the murmur of the motorway would build, going from periodic pulses to one long, languid note. As an instrument, it would have to be a woodwind of sorts, at the droning bass end of the diapason. Now, two vastly different worlds were woven into one, intersecting in their search for pleasure and escape from pain. I thought about each person passing and the worries and wants that drove with them, and I wished them well.

By the time I returned to bed with my tea, the crows had taken charge, their calls always sounding more like commands. The baby magpies had also decided it was mealtime, their continual meeping demanding attention. I could find their insistence amusing because I was not their mother, my responsive smile born from sympathy.

On this day, I did not read or write; I could not concentrate on either pastime. I simply sat with Grief and watched the wind wave through the trees and the see-through screen that shielded my space from mosquitoes. The breeze today was big enough to create gaps in the gauze, and through one flew a dandelion seed. It floated for a while, wandering around the window, its little white parachute following where the wind wanted it to go. I held out my hand with hope, and in a short absence of a breeze, it landed. My heart went out in thanks to this little guest, and I took careful note of its tussled hair and tainted tip. It was a tiny but meaningful meeting, the pappus being picked up again promptly and placed on my curtain in the corner. I wondered what my psych would think of this event. Of course, he would explain it with aerodynamics. I chose to believe the energies at play were far more magical.

It was late morning when the girls lumbered out of their room. Sport had ceased for the season, so the shift into action was sluggish. Not even the promise of spending money at the shops could speed things up. Usually, window shopping was all we could afford, with wish lists stuck on the fridge. The shops were open all day, so the eldest prioritised gossiping with her girlfriends over getting ready. The youngest needed sufficient time for her skincare and so could not be rushed. I was happy to go with the flow, with extraordinarily little energy to be frantic.

Pulling into the shopping centre carpark, I realised my casualness was about to be challenged. It was crammed with cars and suggested the havoc we would meet within. It only took coming down the escalators to begin feeling overwhelmed. I noticed my youngest put her air pods in, a sign she was sheltering herself from the onslaught. We decided to sit for a while at the café to acclimatise to the chaos. The familiarity of this place made it feel a little lighter than the last time we shared this time together. Over coffee, we chatted about colour combinations for the decorations and the project budget. A list was prepared, and a plan was put in place to secure the provisions. Walking three-wide was difficult in this place at the best of times, so we decided to divide and conquer. The girls went together to the fancy places to get the special stuff. I went to the cheaper places and procured the staples; a reasonably priced Christmas tree, lights and lanyards from which we could hang pictures of Nana and Poppy.

I was getting used to Grief being around, but I was still surprised when he shoved me. These bumps came in the most banal places; standing in line for the toilets, putting bags into the trolley, texting a meeting spot to the girls, and waiting for photos to print. Grief did not come with a song and a dance. Sometimes, it provided a punch that would make me gasp over what had gone. Other times, it came as a monotonous pressure, pushing me downwards. In between it was content with just being. I thought about how Grief might be showing up for the girls. I decided to discuss it with them separately, in those sacred times when both their doors and hearts were open.

We were all so glad to make it home; the relative boredom came as a relief. After a late lunch of leftover pizza, we started constructing our Christmas shrine. Colourful chains were connected over windows, with bells and baubles bowing the bridge. Tinsel was tossed over the tree, and pastel teardrops were placed precisely in the gaps. As the action abated, the opportunity arose to offer them Poppy's present. There was the strangest mix of sadness and excitement, and their faces did not know which way to turn. The result was wrestling, which I understood well. It would take time to work through what this meant and to meander through the different shades of sentiment. I told them that their inheritance amount was still unknown and would be settled after the real estate sales. There was plenty of time to plan what we would do with the money, and the most important thing now was to thank dad for all he had done. I prepared his picture and placed it on the tree; this was no simple ornament, but a source of enrichment and expansion.

Encouraged by the energy, I suggested that perhaps this year we also send presents to their aunt, uncle and cousins. They thought it was a great idea, but before we could begin penning down potential purchases, my eldest said," Mum, can I ask a question?" I knew with this introduction I needed to prepare for something immense. She only ever asked to ask when what came next could be unsettling. She used this to check my mindset before leaping in. She was incredibly smart, although her wisdom came at the cost of many monstrous experiences, most imposed upon her by me.

"Why don't we get to see our cousins more often, and why can't we stay with Aunty? What is it with you two?"

She was asking for me to explain the source of the divide. However, I had never tried to synthesise it in my mind. I did not want to begin with, "it's complicated." That would have been considered condescending. Now was as good a time as any to unpack the baggage, so I began by explaining there were many reasons. The first was that we were quite different. We enjoyed diverse things and so didn't have much to connect over. In saying this, though, I was aware that this was likely an effect rather than a cause of the conflict. Digging downwards, I relayed my sister's revelation when she admitted jealousy. But this was only one tiny part of the truth. I testified to the fact that through my addiction, I had caused so much hurt to her, dad and my brother that it was hard to get over. They could relate to this and started to see the responsibility shift sides.

Yet, the picture was still incomplete. It was time to invite Secret to come out of the shadows. Through tears, I told them of my childhood torment. They both came over and embraced me. It felt suddenly that I was being acknowledged as a person, not just an elder. I spelled out that I had surmised my sister had saved me from the situation and that she had been both annoyed and ashamed. In the last few days, I had only found out that the assumptions I had built the gap upon were false. I relayed her experience of being exposed to our cousin's evil exploits and how another girl in the family had also endured this anguish. There was no doubt that these events, even with the best attempts at internalisation, would have contributed to personality problems and crevices between us. Now, though, along with the strength in my sobriety, we were in a new, shared space. I could not assure them that this would accommodate greater alignment, but we had a new way forward. We cuddled and cried together, with Secret, the teenager I met at the airport and the girl in gingham wandering in to be with us. For a moment I felt selfish about sharing such pain, but Secret nodded her assent, the teenager gave me a smile, and the child blew a kiss from her chubby little hands.

My eldest stood up and placed herself in front of us. She wrung her hands, showing she was doing something incredibly hard.

"I have something to tell you, too."

"My boyfriend didn't stop when I asked him too. He just kept going even though I said no."

The youngest let out a wail, expressing just what I was feeling. It was as if two hands had hurtled into my chest, one crushing my heart, the other stirring my stomach. There were no words with which I could respond, and certainly no chance that anything I could say would provide consolation. I knew this from personal experience. For it was not only my daughter's body that had been violated, but her voice. I went over to her and wrapped her in my arms, wishing I had wings. The gaps in my limbs were letting out all I wanted to give. I picked her up like the child she still was and placed her on my lap. I rubbed her back as she sobbed. As the crying ceased, she laid back into me and looked for a long time to where Secret sat. I wondered if my secret was now keeping company with hers.

There were so many things I wanted to know, but now was not the time or the place. Any demands would be made to redress my own damage, not hers. I could feel Anger amassing its armaments, but I closed the door to its company. He would be of no help here. She had already walked past the place I was at now and coming at her screaming from behind would surely only scare her more. The youngest came and put her arms around us, filling in the spaces that distressed me. Maybe you don't need wings, I thought, just multiple arms.

The youngest broke the heavy silence with a wonderful blend of humour and heart.

"Do you want me to kill him for you. I can. I have been practicing karate!"

The chuckles were honest, helping me ease the embrace and endorse her movement. My mind turned to managing the dissociation dancing in front of me, attempting to mute it so I could offer adequate attention.

"I think I would like to finish the decorations now", she said wiping away the tears. We joined her, blowing up the inflatables I had tried to convince them to cull from the Christmas list. They thought they were cute, and I came to agree. The synchronicity of now breathing deeply to bring them to life was not lost on me.

We wandered through the evening, too full of lunch, to think of more than toast and ice cream for dinner. At bedtime, I went to tuck the girls in, sitting first with my eldest. I thanked her for telling me about something I knew was so difficult. I congratulated her for her bravery and begged her not to bury herself under the blame. I needed her to know that she was not faulty and that, somehow, she needed to find a way to forgive herself. We discussed how sinister Shame was, and we both cried again. I knew she had learnt much from this and that, moving forward, she needed to decide what to cling to and leave behind. I asked if she wanted me to approach the parents or the boyfriend to address the issue directly. She declined. I asked her if she would like to talk about it more with me, maybe tomorrow. She declined again. Then, I suggested that this would benefit from a walk-through with her counsellor. She agreed and I affirmed I would make a booking for the first available appointment.

My own bed did not feel so luscious that night. I longed for it as always, but it was drenched in discomfort. While I had preached to my daughter about not feeling faulty, I felt like a complete failure. I should have made sure she was confident with consent when she started dating and protested to the boy's parents when I saw them exiting from a closed door one day at pickup. I should have stipulated to the parents that our rule was for doors to stay open during visits, and this could have been prevented. I had not done all I should have to protect her, the one I professed to love.

Now I was also delegating my duty of mending the mutilations, transferring this task to her therapist. I let Anger loose, and it told me that I should ignore my daughter's wishes and accost the parents. I could already see the look on the mother's face when I told her about her prized son's imperfections. It was the same one I pictured on my aunt's face when I role-played revealing her son's abuse. I was planning the path forward, preparing to pounce the next day, when Angel appeared. He lay in the space between Grief, Anger and me, waved one wing slowly above me, creating a cooling wind and a diversion from my ire. When its work was done, it settled around my spine, offering sympathy and support. Angel's hand stroked my eyebrows, and he kissed my tears.

"It begins with you, Juno. Do not just tell, for your words will soon be washed away. Show her how it is done. Prepare for her a path."

I reached out my hand to hold his arm, seeking strength in his solid shape. The armour was not there. Instead, I felt flesh firmed from many fights covered by soft, loose cloth. His face was radiant, illuminated by the light of the full moon, and I finally understood the word, Divine. We lay looking at each other for a long time. I was longing to see more and know more of Angel. But as much as I tried to hold onto this moment, brief blinks became extended until, eventually, there was no energy left to open my eyes. Without sight, I shifted my attention to the feeling of being loved by Angel, and I begged Memory for this never to be forgotten.

I'M SORRY JUNO

Chapter 12

The next morning began with the birds. But they were background noise to the buzz going on in my brain, and were soon hushed by sheets of rain. There was no sun streaming in, only a grey haze. The weather was certainly a case of as within, so without. While it was gloomy though, it also came with a sense of gladness. It relieved me of much home maintenance and permitted me to spend the day inside and in peaceful pursuits. We had nothing on that day, so the clouds were not inconvenient. They created a cosy container in which we could come to terms with things. This day, of no pressures, was precious.

I rolled over, away from Grief, and watched the rain place a translucent curtain across the trees, and the puddles on my deck get pounded and expand into one another. And I watched the windowpane, waiting to see the daring drops that would speed downwards. My girls thought I was weird when I did a voiceover of the raindrops on the car window, singing, "yippee" as they slid down the glass. Today, though, they did not shriek joyfully but let out a more serious, "excuse me" as they sailed past those drops still stuck.

This scene sucked me back to the long car trips I took with my family as a child to the big smoke. These journeys were rare, and not enjoyed with screens but with novels, puzzles and colouring books. There was also very little space with the three kids trapped together in the back seat. I was wedged against one window, my sister the other, allowing the wind on her face to calm her stomach. Inevitably, though, there was a stop along the way to let her spew, usually sometime after the stop for lunch where we had soggy egg sandwiches. On the days it rained, we all chose a window and studied the glass for drips about to descend. When two would start a race, we would rapidly take bets on which one would reach the bottom first. A tally was kept, and winners were announced as we pulled back into our driveway.

But this day was not one for such excitement. It was a day for introspection, identifying what was truly important, and setting intentions. I made tea as mindfully as possible and lit a candle and incense to support me in my considerations. These were not done to summon any spirit or stir any soul but my own.

The tea flowed warmly down my throat, and I welcomed it as a faithful friend. It would not be long before there would be more life in these limbs and optimism in my mind. I put my hand out to allow the curls of incense smoke to stroke my palm. I was sure I felt a tingle as we touched. My psych would readily explain this event away as being from adjusting blood flow. But I believed otherwise and offered it a greeting and gratitude for its generosity.

As the tea smoothed the terrain of my thoughts and stirred my senses, I began to figure out what was needed from me that day, not in terms of tasks but of temperament. As Angel had known, the reality was that my girls looked to me as a guide for how to react. There may be days off from duties, but there was never any downtime in being on display. They took stock of not what I said but what I did. Today, then, needed to be a day where I let Love lead.

Today's priority was being true to my purpose – to pass it on. I reinforced this aspiration with reading, selecting whatever spiritual text was stacked on my bedside table. I seemed to so easily default to the deception that I spent my days alone. The pile of books strewn around my house told a different story; that I was surrounded by a world of wise well-wishers.

Suspecting that the girls might soon arise, I snuck downstairs and made pancake mix. Sure, they were quite capable of doing it themselves. Yet I knew how much they appreciated it already being done, and today, preparing pancakes seemed a pursuit well aligned with my plan.

My eldest entered the kitchen with what appeared to be a combination of caution and reluctance like she was on reconnaissance. Perhaps she was wondering if I had remembered her revelation and whether I had a new response in store. She knew I had the night to think things through and may have awoken with a plan of attack. Her tension seemed to ease when I embraced her and kissed her head.

"How are you honey?"

"I'm OK."

"Did you get a good sleep?"

"Sort of."

The discussion continued in sporadic, short sentences, typical for the teenage years and more so in the mornings. At least this was a bit better than the solo syllables I used to get from my brother. I considered this exchange an icebreaker, a warm-up. Pushing the mind muscles too early could lead to an injury, to her attitude, and to my chances for more comprehensive conversations.

We parked on the lounge with pancakes, mine a mass of Nutella and berries, hers veiled in vegemite with ice cream on the side. Between bites, we began exploring ideas for presents for her aunt, uncle and cousins. Eye-contact was almost non-existent. It was far easier to engage with what she was eating. Perhaps she did not want to encourage discussions about her ex-boyfriend. Or was she ashamed of her secret? She likely blamed herself for burdening me, believing she was a bad daughter. I had been there, and it was a terrific torment.

"Honey, thank you for telling me about what happened with your boyfriend. It must have been really hard to do that, but I really appreciate you trusting me with it."

While still staring at her food she gave a series of nods.

"Can I chat to you later about what happened? I don't want to know the details unless you want to share. I would just really appreciate your advice on what we do next, for your situation and mine."

I hoped these words and the calm they conveyed gave her some confidence that I was coping.

"Maybe later?"

"Sure. How about I check in with you this afternoon?"

She agreed and returned to stabbing her spoon into the ice cream, creating a sweet, cold mush. We continued with present planning and decided on some birthday stone jewellery sets for the girls and a garish, gem-studded keyring for my brother. The latter was over the top, but we were sure that he would see the challenge that came with it. Would he be brave enough to bear some bling? We decided to send it along with some scratchies, just like mum would have done, and a card that said, "We saw this and thought of you :)."

This sneakiness started some smiles, and the room felt a little lighter.

It was not long before the eldest and youngest swopped places. The first went back to bed, and the second finally came from it. By then, pancakes were an early lunch, and I worked with the youngest to find a place to buy the presents we had picked. While I did the online ordering, we discussed the inheritance money, and she rattled off a whole range of ideas of how she would like to use it when she turned 18. The plans involved lots of travel, and the thought of tripping to new and exciting places brought further brightness.

When my phone rang, I was more than a little perturbed. I was quarantining this day to let our heads and hearts recover, and now our beautiful bubble had been broken. It was a number I did not know, which, on most days meant I would not have answered. Such calls either requested my participation in a senseless marketing survey or were a utility service chasing payment. I didn't want to know about the first, and I already knew about the latter, so there was no need to converse. However, we were still in quite a state of flux from the funeral, and being a weekend, it could be a friendly voice, so I took the chance to answer.

It was my aunt. Not the chubby, cuddly mother of the monster, but the thin, stylish one with perfect diction. I gave a generous greeting and moved onto the deck to avoid disturbing my daughter's TV time having background noise compete with our conversation. Her voice was low, slow and sad. She was weary, and her words were only just above a whisper. Her baby brother was gone, and she was hurting. She had loved my dad desperately and doted on him as an adoring big sister. While we did not meet often, each time we did, she talked about her brother as a boy, how he had almost died as a baby, and how he recovered to become a mischievous but warm-hearted man. While our lives were lived very separately, they were spun together by this shared sadness.

"I am sorry I didn't get to see you again before you left," she said. "I wanted to see if you made it home OK. "

"Yes, I did thanks, the trip went well."

"How are you, Juno?"

"I'm doing OK, thanks." I wanted to say I was so glad to be home but hesitated, unsure if this may be hurtful.

"How are you, Aunty? You sound so tired."

"Yes I am. I have seen so many passings, and each seems to compound the pain. Getting older does not help either, knowing that it will be my turn soon to say goodbye."

There was not much I could say in response, and I was pleased that an awkward silence was averted by an additional asking.

"And how are the girls?"

"They are as good as they can be." Given that she was overcome with her own grief, I did not see any need to expand on how it showed up for them.

"They are so beautiful, Juno. You should be so proud."

This suggestion turned my stomach.

I was unsure why I had such an aversion to Pride. It seemed like such an innocuous noun, naming the intangible satisfaction, the internal reward that comes with invested effort. For me, though, contemplating Pride came with a complete sense of disgust. Its name being voiced caused a visceral reaction and the desire to dry retch. Pride was something I neither deserved nor wanted and must be kept as far away as possible. I had caused too many problems to be proud of my life. And in addiction recovery, Pride was admonished as the predecessor of complacency and a precursor to relapse. In my mind, it was associated with disaster and distress, and I wanted nothing to do with it. However, I did put a placeholder in mind to sit with Pride again later and listen to what it had to say.

For now, though, there was no way I could be proud of what I had achieved as a parent. No one who knew the hurt I put my family through would suggest such a thing. I could not take credit for healing the wounds that I, myself, had wrought. Besides, my girls were not something I owned, a product of my making, to be promoted and upheld like a prize. I was honoured to help them through the hellish gates of growing up. They were not trophies but people exploring their passions. Pride was a nice sentiment, but what they really needed was a safe place to rest, retreat and restore energy for their next expedition. I was hopeful the home we had created would provide such a haven. While the word made me feel sick, I understood the intention and did not wish to insult my aunt with my grim inference, instead saying,

"Yes, they are truly gorgeous."

"Well, I wanted to let you know that I am here if you need anything. With your mum and dad gone – if you have any difficulties – please call. I would love to be able to help wherever I can."

The complex concerns with my own children had completely overshadowed the fact that I was now an orphan. Although this did not bring any sense of overwhelm. They had left me so much, and I was accustomed to managing things alone.

"I also wanted to ask about something."

Her voice went from sympathetic to serious, and my mood went from flat to fraught.

"Do you remember what you told me once on the phone, about Brett?"

I felt my whole body begin to burn. Oh my god. I had hoped that drunken dialogue had been forgotten. It happened one Sunday afternoon, years ago, when I was alone. After a few chardonnays, I was chatty and wanted to connect, so I set about making a slew of phone calls. I have tried to console myself by claiming that Secret had just slipped out, but that was delusional and deceptive. In truth, I had intended to take any opportunity to tell, even before I had started talking.

"I am so sorry I burdened you with that Aunty...so sorry."

I saw Shame sneak up and sit beside me.

"Honestly, Juno, I was at the time too. In fact, I was quite worried, and really did not know what to do with it until yesterday. Jennifer came to see me and told me a shocking story. It seems your sister shared with her the horrible experiences you both had with Brett. She was so overwrought she had to talk and tell me what happened to her too."

"Oh gosh, Aunty, I am so sorry."

"I am not anymore, Juno. In fact, you telling your truth has allowed me to finally help my daughter. It explains so very much. I only wish I had known earlier, and I could have eased her troubles and let her know she was not alone."

The last sentences were broken by sobs.

"Aunty, I have spent years imagining how I could have said something. But we grew up in a time and a place that offered little support. We could never talk about those things, and to even try raising the subject would have been met with terror. I am just so glad that Jennifer can finally share this with you."

"Well, the question is now, Juno, what are we going to do about it? We are in a bit of a bind, aren't we? We can't involve Brett's mum; it would break her heart."

Like my parents, Aunty had slipped swiftly from sadness and sympathy into problem-solving mode. I wondered if this was a particular gift of her generation. While consideration and compassion were still present, action was seen as the all-important next step.

"I agree. It would just lead to her blaming herself and that won't help anyone."

"Speaking of blame. You know what happened to you is not your fault."

"Thanks, Aunty, and yes, I know this in theory. I don't quite understand why it is so hard to believe in practice. It's kind of like as women we are hard-wired to take on responsibilities that are not our own. I have been thinking about it a lot, and it seems ever since the story of Eve we have been led to believe we are the bad ones, and that we must bear the burden of breaking the rules. We are still living with the wounds imposed on women way back in time. We became the scapegoat for those men who could not deal with their own human nature. We have a lot of unlearning to do to truly live equally."

Suddenly, I thought of how often I said sorry to others in a day, and just for the slightest of things. Stepping in front of someone in the street, making it first to the water fountain at work and leaving the other person waiting. It was also the first word I said when I asked for help in a store. There was never any personal injury, just the possibility of causing the other inconvenience. And yet, with this single word, sorry, I seemed to take responsibility for their reaction and accountability for their answers. I had offered them the right to be frustrated and annoyed by my actions and took on the debt of any displeasure. What was often perceived as merely being polite had an ominous outcome.

This was so different from Angel's apology, a sincere acknowledgement of my pain. And my constant and superficial "sorry" to strangers was vastly inferior to the honest offerings I had made to my aunt. My ongoing apologies in public places were superfluous and insidious. They were a subtle suggestion that my existence should be excused and that my needs may be negated. I made a mental note to bring more awareness to the words and to spend some more time thinking about the beliefs behind them. But now was not the time. My Aunt needed action.

"Jen and your sister don't not want me to do anything. Jen has promised me she has sought out help in the past and will again when she needs it. I want to respect her wishes but it goes against my grain. I am hoping she will change her mind and that she will allow me to intervene. I want the chance to face Brett as the mother of the girl he abused and let him know he is being held to account. But I will abide by her instructions."

Exactly at that moment, I heard the echo of my own heart. My Aunt held a mirror, and I could clearly see the mangled mess of my emotions. I could no longer hold the heartache. I did mute it, though, managing to maintain silent tears.

"But what about you? Did you want me to call him on your behalf? Juno, I think at the very least you deserve an apology."

"You are right, Aunty. If the apology was honest, it may help. Any given simply for compliance though would be cruel and I would be worried if you were involved this is all it would be. I will be honest and tell you I have struggled with this for so many years, trying to decide if I should demand one. But I have come to think that's not how healing works. Instead, I am focusing on forgiving myself and this is taking far more effort than I could have ever imagined. I would like to move forward Aunty, but on my own. I deeply appreciate your offer, but this is very much a personal journey."

"Seeing you at the funeral, Juno, and hearing you now, I am comfortable with that. A few years ago, I was getting prepared to step in. I was really worried about what you were going to do."

"So was I for a while."

I felt no need to admit that this period had only ended a few days ago, and the path of forgiveness I had chosen was still firming.

"I just hope whatever Jen decides to do will help bring peace. Please pass on my warmest wishes and let her know she is welcome to call any time."

We parted with the agreement to check in again in a few weeks or beforehand if there were any developments. I stayed outside for a while, deciding I really needed a debrief. There were so many conflicting emotions churning around and through me. There was Comfort coming in for a cuddle, while at the same time, Sorrow was showing me a slideshow, flipping through the faces of my daughters, Jen, my aunt and my sister. Grief was the ghost gliding around us while Responsibility watched, waiting by the window. Hope sat there, too, holding hands with Faith. I could not concentrate on a single sensation. Still, it did not feel like a confused cacophony, more like a collegiate community. There was nothing any of them needed at that moment, just the permission to abide in this place. When all seemed content, I went back inside and lay out on the lounge, indulging in some binge-viewing before bothering my eldest.

I could feel myself drifting off and decided to succumb to my body's own sense. When I awoke, the shadows had shifted, and the youngest had left. It took me a while to fully awaken, washing my face and making a coffee to force some momentum. I made my eldest an iced version with whipped cream and delivered it, and me, beside her. She had sent me some reels earlier that day, full of fantastic food ideas, so we snuggled and surveyed her suggested feast. From recipes we meandered onto swimwear and then headed into hairstyles. We had wandered into the world of cats riding around on vacuum cleaners when I decided we were warm enough for a deeper discussion.

"How are you doing, honey?"

This query settled the smile on her face, and I felt her form tense. She knew this was the start of our serious conversation, and she was bracing herself for what lay before her. There was a second in which I thought about changing tack and starting a shopping list of supplies to support her in making the reels a reality. This choice point came often when I was with my children. I could ignore an issue, keep everyone smiling, or address it and create angst. The first path was so easy and certainly reduced my own stress. The second meant doling out discomfort to all residents as the slamming doors and sulks spread their stink across the entire site. So, I chose my confrontations carefully, considering the pros and cons of each choice. Yes, I could let this go and allow the girl to continue without further interference from her mother. But what message would that send? This was not something that could or should be swept under the carpet. Its implications were too important. There was also a magical opportunity being presented for us to heal, separately, together. I did not want this missed because of my own timidity.

"I am so sorry, Lainey. And don't you dare say it's OK. Because what happened to you is not OK."

I kept my words soft, slow and gentle, attempting to replicate Angel's tone.

"Did you want to tell me what happened?"

"No."

"I understand."

"I know you do."

Those four simple words created an explosion of pain and peace, and I was pushed forward to put my arms around her. There was Understanding here, and where there was Understanding, there was Love.

"Lainey, do you think I am a bad person for what happened to me?"

"No, of course not." She looked surprised that I even asked this question.

"Do you think you are a bad person for what happened to you?"

She was silent, and I could see her trying to accommodate conflicting approaches, one of compassion for me and another of condemnation for her. I understood this infighting intimately, as it was also inside me, diminishing each day but decidedly still present.

"Do you think I was right to share my secret?

"Of course."

"Do you think you were right to share what happened to you?"

Again, silence, and I sensed another struggle.

"Lainey, what you are learning right now is a lesson that may take your whole life. You are worthy of the same understanding and care that you are giving to me. You deserve the same love that you show me each day. If you can carry one light out of this darkness honey, then let it be that of self-compassion. Sweetheart, you have the absolute freedom to spend your life punishing yourself, but I can tell you from my experience that this will never bring you peace, and in fact, will only lead to you hurting more people along the way. I know you truly care for everyone around you, but to do that well you need to care for yourself first."

She cuddled around me, confirming her acceptance of the concept.

"If it is OK with you, I would like to get a book on self-compassion that can explain it so much better than I can and shows you some tools to try out."

She nodded her assent. Even if the book sat on her shelf, it would be a start.

"Perfect."

I paused to appreciate the preciousness of this moment, turning my attention to the tender touch of the child in my arms. As we began to breathe together, tears began to form, and the pressure of her head touched my heart, a testament to my truth. I used this strength to step forward past Fear.

"I know you don't want to say anything, Lainey. And I really get that. What worries me, though, is without saying anything, he may think that his actions are OK. They are not, and he needs to know that. Lainey, I love you for your kindness, and I know you don't want to hurt anyone. But letting him go on without saying anything is cruel to him and to you. He might continue overstepping boundaries with other girls, and so by saying nothing, you are condoning his cruelty. Saying something now is actually being kind to him and may prevent others from going through the same situation."

I let that idea sink in for a few seconds.

"And Lainey, just as importantly, you have let your voice be invalidated. It may seem like a one-off occurrence now, but it does set a precedent. You can try and repress it, but it will just sit inside of you and rot. You are free to try and forget this ever happened, but you also have a responsibility to your own heart, your own values and your own voice, and they will keep haunting you with regrets until you help them out."

I felt a power spread from my heart and through each limb. This was a revelation not merely read, a realisation not rote learned from another's preaching. It emanated from my experience, and at once, I knew the meaning of the word real.

"Lainey, I know there is a lot to deal with here. So, please take time, care for yourself, come and cuddle whenever you want to. You are so loved my little Lainey, for all that you are."

A few moments passed, and then the wings of a butterfly outside brought a wisp of Angel's inspiration.

"All those years ago, Lainey, I feel like I lost my voice too. Not just because of my cousin, but by the whole way we were brought up back then. But what happened with Brett played a part, and I am thinking about writing him a letter."

"Why? And what would you say?"

"Both good questions, honey. Why? Not to cast blame or let him know I am angry. I want to reclaim my voice; to let him know that I know what he did was wrong, and that it has caused hurt. I want to give him the chance to apologise, even though I really don't expect it. I think I want to let him know that I have forgiven him. It will be a tricky letter to craft. You are so great with ideas. Do you think I could get your help?"

We parted while I went to get paper and a pen and then reunited as a duo, we documented dot points that I would turn later into text. There were only a handful, but each was huge and heavy. The wonderful girl suggested a very fitting ending - a reminder to care for Poppy's cows. That sense of closure caused me to clasp my arms around her and affirm a newfound sense of acceptance. I thanked Lainey and lay beside her while we watched some otters eating cabbage – cute, amusing and surprisingly calming.

"Mum, I think I'm going to go for a career in medicine. Maybe paediatrics. It might be tricky to get the marks, but with Poppy' help, I will have the money."

"Honey, you can be anything you want if you put your heart into it. I know the sick kids would be super lucky to have you as their doctor."

A kiss on the forehead denoted the conclusion of this chapter, and I wandered into my youngest's room for a casual check-in.

"How are you going my marvellous Maya?"

The regular response to my silliness was a side-eye and a sneer. It was a game we played, and I was pleased to see she still had enough energy to partake in it.

"What are you up to in here?"

"Just putting together my Christmas wish list."

"Ah, I see. So, are you going to max out Santy's credit card with this one?"

The reaction to this question was a mischievous grin.

"Come, I'll show you."

She signalled for me to sit beside her on the bed and showed me all the items in the multiple shopping carts. She did have a wonderful sense of style, and I told her so. It was an automatic action for me to spy on her scars and see how they were healing. The laser treatment had done a terrific job of calming their appearance. She had a wish granted early this Christmas, now being able to swim with confidence. The process to this stage, though, had been horrific. My first full sighting had been with the specialist, and it took all my strength to smother my shock. There was a lattice over her legs, constructed from confusion and painted with her pain.

The specialist did not share my surprise, advising that at least ten per cent of kids wore the same wounds, and what he saw was not unusual. This comment was meant to provide consolation but only created more sadness. I sat there and watched as the laser wrought more wounding, this time with the intent of inspiring healing. In the end, her thighs were a red, raw network. Yet this was the most relaxed and positive I had seen her in a long time. I tried to open my heart to the extent of the horror, but my well-practised protections were not ready to resign just yet. They held their positions, allowing me only to peek behind the curtain. Still, this was progress.

She took my paper and pen, wrote down her list, and we tallied the total.

"Only a thousand dollars?"

And so, a new game began when we pretended that this budget was reasonable and that we were one of the rich girls from the TV shows.

"I am sure you can do better than that!"

Then came the fun of finding the most expensive, eccentric items that we could judge to bring even more joy. There were bodysuits with built-in nipples, jewelled joggers, crocodile leather clutches, and gold teeth grills. We compiled a character covered in these treasures and decided her name was Tiara.

"Mum, what's for dinner?"

Lainey yelled from her room and made me realise how hungry I was too.

"Let's do burger bowls tonight."

"Yippee. Yes please."

I fussed around frantically, fixed on getting dinner done and dusted. This was our routine on Sunday nights when Poppy would call. Eating and cleaning would cease by 7pm so that we could converse with a sense of calm. It took some time for me to realise that tonight would be different and that there was no longer a dinner deadline. In a way, I regretted this new-found relaxation.

When the time did come, I went and put on the Christmas Lights. Memory and Love joined us as we wrote down the things we loved about Poppy and slid them in behind his photo on the tree. I asked if there was anything they wanted to know about Nana, and the questions came quickly.

"What was her favourite food?" Of course, this was Lainey's enquiry.

"Ah, that is easy. Anything with cream. She would make porridge and smother it with brown sugar and cream for breakfast. Then at nighttime she would have a bowl of stewed apples soaked in cream. Surprisingly, she was as thin as a rake and had perfect cholesterol!"

"What was her hobby?"

"Well, she didn't really have much of one. She was working most of the time. But she did love to knit. She made most of our jumpers as kids. She also cooked the most incredible date puddings at Christmas time and delivered all to the neighbours. I do remember she always wanted to try spinning wool, but she never got the chance."

"Did she do any sport?"

"Yep, Nana was an awesome cricketer! She played in the local league, but there was no chance for girls to go further back then. I am sure she would have loved watching you run around playing footy. She would have thought what you girls can do now is fantastic."

"What was her heritage?"

"Irish through and through. I have her to thank for my freckles and curls."

"How many brothers and sisters did she have again?"

"There were nine. It was a huge family in one tiny cottage. You have more second-cousins that you could count. Maybe we will get to meet them all one day. A lot of Nana's brothers and sisters have died, but the ones still here would love to tell you more."

We were too tired to keep talking, so Maya put on her crime drama. We had been binge-viewing the entire series every weekend for months, and we had become remarkably close to the characters. At the end of this episode, one man is slipping in and out of consciousness, clinging to life after being tortured. He imagines his dead father standing with him in a field, offering advice on how to surmount his suffering. The father states that he is so proud of the man. These words, though, instead of bringing solace, bring misery. This bit made me pay attention for this feeling was all too familiar. This was no longer just a piece of fiction, but a replica of my reality.

Then, the man pleads with his father, trying to understand how he could possibly be proud of him. He has failed this mission, and now, with his death, he would have also failed his family. The father simply replies that he has been watching for years as his son found ways to turn his pain into strength and how he passed this on to others. This is the success of which the father is proud.

This scene was an act of synchronicity, and I wondered whether some spiritual sages had pulled strings with this programming. I sent a silent "thank you" to whoever was involved in this because these were exactly the words I needed to hear; they crept past my protectors and pinned open the curtain to let more light through.

We needed to balance the solemn with the superficial, so we watched some selfish rich girls flying around the world on private jets and buying up all the things we had made fun of in the afternoon. They took selfies at all the tourist sites, not just one but several, and even more as they walked away. When they tired of one place, they had their people pack them up, and the pilot transported them to the next photo opportunity. It was not long before we had our fill of such fantastic folly and went our separate ways to sleep.

Looking out at the night sky, I thought about what I would do if I had wings. Where would I fly to? What would I go and see? There was so much of this world that I wanted to know more about, and how wonderful it would be to experience the places and people in person. I flowed with this freedom for a while, soaring between India and Egypt, across to Antarctica and gliding across the Grand Canyon. I drifted down past Uluru and then to the fairy forests in Ireland. There was no plan for this expedition. I followed the whim of my wonderings.

Sitting, surrounded by the spirits of my ancestors, I considered the remaining half of this honour. If I had the freedom to land in each place, what responsibility must I fulfil before I leave? Perhaps the responsibility was to provide the same respect that they granted me. All these sites allowed me to see them in all their different degrees of life and decay. They permitted me to touch both their perfections and flaws. Maybe the greatest regard I could provide was reciprocity; as I saw them, let them see me. As I touched them, let them touch me. My responsibility was to turn a taking into a sharing. There was a difference between being a witness and being with; the latter is what each place wanted. In my imagination I snuggled up to one of the gentle giant trees. I ran my palm against the rough bark, finding the sensation and meaning magical. Then I fell asleep against its trunk, listening to its internal world and letting it listen to mine.

I slept in the next morning, missing the first birds and opening my eyes only at breakfast time for the baby magpies. I found their high-pitched cries hilarious and wondered whether their mothers were equally amused. It was always easier to be impartial when the child was not your own. In her place, I suspected I would surely be irritated. This morning, though, I sought their inspiration. They used their voice so that all could know their needs and to have them met. They sang their heart out and would not stop until they had been heard. It was who they were, and they made no apologies for what they wanted.

That was the part I found hardest about my daughter's experience; her voice not being heard, and her needs invalidated. Her wings had been clipped, and her voice suppressed, but it was time for her to sing. Look to nature, and you will find the answers you seek. Thank you, baby magpies. I have received your message.

I knew what I must do, but first, I needed to swim. The pump started pushing the nighttime leaves towards the drain, and I dived in. The water was delicious, crisp enough to stir my senses, yet warm enough to feel welcoming. I stretched my limbs and sailed across the surface, diving down to pick up the leaves that had drowned and delivering them to shore. The sense of weightlessness was liberating, and I found the flow against my flesh fascinating. I could have stayed there for hours, practising sharing myself with all that surrounded me; the water and the wind, the insects and the trees, the sun and the sky. But on the next surfacing, I was greeted by a great white feather right in front of my face. It must have come from a cockatoo, the bird I commended for its authentic screech, and which I considered a personal champion. It sat atop the water, with it but not subsumed by it. I spent a few moments simply watching it before acting on its call. I picked up this precious portent and, making mini puddles along the way, placed it on the Buddha head in my bedroom. Then I dried myself off, primed my laptop and launched into my letter; the letter a long time in the making.

That afternoon, I asked Lainey if she would like to read it, and she did, in silence. The only response she gave was a gigantic hug. I did not ask for specifics; this was my assignment, and I was satisfied with it. It was short and simple. It spoke of harm and hurt. It spoke of forgetfulness and forgiveness. It spoke with Angel's compassion and advocated for the cows.

"I've decided I'm going to speak to my counsellor tomorrow about sending a text to my ex-boyfriend."

"That sounds like fantastic idea. Good on you, honey."

That would be tomorrow. The same day, my letter would begin its journey.

The last week of school for the year came and went, with Angel popping in randomly. Sometimes, he would come to sit with me as I worked at home, wandering around the garden and sitting to watch the spiders. His company was comforting, his silence presence settling. Other times, he would turn up as I fell asleep, stroking my hair and kissing my forehead. In between, I would spy butterflies bedecked in browns and bronzes and bowed to them as they passed. I was sure if my psych found out about these behaviours, he would up my medication, so I hid these new secrets willingly.

On the first day of the holidays, Lainey, Maya and I sat and scoped out how we would spend our time. Just then, I received a text from my sister. Our Aunty, my mum's sister, was having a family reunion on New Year's Day. All mum's side of the family was invited, and she asked if I was interested. The inquiry did not come with any offer of accommodation at my sister's house, but it was not expected; that would have been one step too far for where we were at. The girls would be with their father for Christmas, but it would be possible for us to drive down a few days afterwards and arrive there in time.

The girls were excited about the prospect of a road trip. It meant a few days of take away for every meal, new sights, car naps and mischief in musty motels. The routine was well-rehearsed; While I went to bed early, giddy from the travel, the girls would stay up all night giggling. The next day, they would show me the photos they had sneakily taken of me sleeping. There was a vast variety of versions, all with different filters and captions, and all shared with their friends. My fury was a false façade and added to the fun.

Was I up to reconnecting with relatives I had rejected for so long? Would it be pleasant, or would we just feel out of place again? I was tormented by my motto, "You don't know until you try". However, I did know that I was still exhausted from the events of the past few weeks and was not sure whether hours behind the wheel would be safe. At this time of year, we could not afford to fly either. So, I sent my thanks and told her to put us down as a tentative, and I would confirm in the coming days.

On Christmas Eve, the girls' dad came to pick them up. Over coffee and chocolate, we caught up on how our respective families were doing. He restated how sorry he was that he could not attend dad's funeral. We confirmed plans for pickup in two days, and I planted a kiss on each of the girls' foreheads, another thing from Angel that I wanted to pass on.

Walking back from the road, I stopped at the letterbox, usually barren or lived in by one lonely bill. Today it held something very different; An envelope undersized for utilities and with a handwritten address. I thought of my aunts who shared my mother's habit of bringing happiness on birthdays. One or two cards always came for me in the lead-up to Christmas, although for how much longer, I could not be sure. I turned the envelope over to see which lovely lady this one was from but was taken aback by the senders' details. It was from Brett.

I felt the whole-body blush come back and saw Expectation and Doubt appear before me, eagerly glancing at the correspondence I held. They were both calling me to rip it open and read it at once. But this letter deserved much more regard. I walked them all back inside, put the letter on the table to rest and went outside to watch the spiders. Oh my gosh, was that a straight line in their web? Life is always full of surprises! And then I wondered, if I asked, whether Angel may join me for the reading. Regardless, I knew whatever the response within, it was a gift.

I'M SORRY JUNO

.

Meet Belinda Tobin

Belinda Tobin is a researcher, author, producer, and avid explorer of the human experience with all its challenges and complexities. Her works span fiction, non-fiction, poetry, tv series and film. However, they all share a common purpose, to foster a more conscious, compassionate and connected future.

Find out more about Belinda and her projects at www.belindatobin.com.

I'M SORRY JUNO

About Bel House Books

At Bel House Books, we are dedicated to stories that do more than entertain — they heal. Our collection features narratives where authors have courageously confronted trauma and painful pasts, transforming their hurt into pathways toward healthier, more hopeful futures. These books explore the people they have been, and through the characters they craft, and the wisdom of their words create new perspectives on who they can become.

Here are the available titles from Bel House Books.

THE LOVE LIFE OF A
CHAMELEON

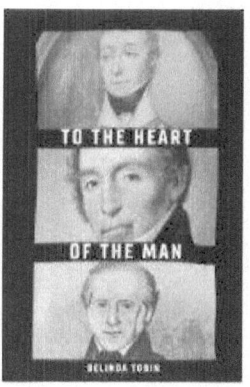

I'M SORRY JUNO

Read On

The Love Life of A Chameleon

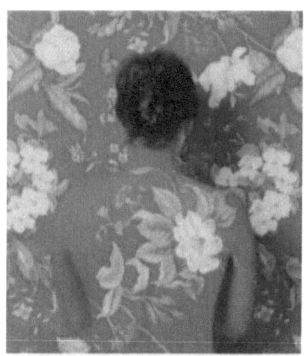

THE LOVE LIFE OF A
CHAMELEON

BELINDA TOBIN

Embark on a brutal yet beautiful journey of self-discovery.

Nora is a capable, proud, professional woman standing on her own two feet and climbing to the position of Partner. She is also now a patient in a psych ward, pulled apart by her longing for love but her inability to accept it. Nora has two great fears: being alone and facing the reality that her life is a facade. Now, she is being forced to confront both.

In this brutal yet beautiful tale, we live with Nora as she works through the consequences of her childhood experiences and the expansive sequence of self-destructive choices. We listen as she begins to comprehend how she has used her sexuality as a tool to conquer, control and avoid true connection. We witness her understanding of how the environments she has endured have left her with many scars, some seen, some buried beneath layers of lies.

Nora decides not to return to the life that led her to the hospital but to a solitary sanctuary, her mother's home filled with memories of what true love looks like. She finds a firm footing, friendship, inspiring projects and the unconditional love of a little girl. But she also carries with her ingrained harmful habits and problematic self-beliefs. Will she resist the pull to join another toxic partnership simply to avoid being a spinster?

Through Nora's story, we get to reflect on the rainbow of our lives, each colour calling us to appreciate the conflict between fitting in and finding oneself, knowing who you are and who you are not, and the tussle between convenient deceit and deep truth. As Nora charts and celebrates her complexity, we are also guided to gain a sense of self-compassion for our own challenges and to find the courage to create our own homes where there is honesty, health, happiness and hope.

Read On

Crucifixus

Between Silence and Song

Crucifixus is a compelling historical novel that vividly presents the emotional and physical toll of gender trauma in the 17th century. It was a time when women were silenced and forced to be subservient to men and when men caused suffering through their declared superiority and hidden insecurities. Because women were not allowed to sing in Church, boys were sacrificed for their voices, becoming castratos for the Glory of God and the gratification of His flock.

Crucifixus chronicles the tragic journey of Paulo, a seven-year-old boy chosen by Church officials to become a castrato for the choir. Torn from his family and forced into a world of brutal discipline, Paulo finds solace in music, achieving fleeting fame in private operas. Yet, the cost of his voice is steep, leaving him to battle both physical pain and emotional desolation.

Paulo's solitude is softened by a tender and sincere bond with Contessa Vittoria, a noblewoman who offers him comfort and curiosity. But when the impossible dreams of marriage crumble, and his body begins turning against him, he turns to opium, spiralling into despair.

Paulo's story intertwines with that of his family — his brother Antonio, who is angered by the fragility of women and abhors castratos; his brother Luca, who encounters the toxic power of patrons; his sister Francesca, who envies his chance to sing; and their mother, who sent Paulo away in the hope of a better future. Their choices reverberate through society, leaving a lasting impact.

Through richly evocative prose, Crucifixus offers a moving portrayal of the devastating impact of societal expectations founded upon fear. It examines the ripple effects of gendered suffering, exploring the struggles of a family torn apart by choices made in the name of faith and survival.

Crucifixus is one of many untold stories of the nearly half a million boys who were forever altered to serve the Church's music program between the 16th and 18th centuries. In the end, the question remains: Can forgiveness ever heal the wounds of the past?

For more titles go to:
www. heart-led.pub/bel-house-books